A To

MW00915902

A Nuts about Nuts Cozy Mystery Series

Cindy Bell

Copyright © 2016 Cindy Bell

All rights reserved.

ISBN-13: 978-1537498225

ISBN-10: 1537498223

Table of Contents

Chapter One

It was a beautiful dream. The kind that she never wanted to wake up from. She stood under a waterfall, the water cool against her skin. Sunlight shimmered through the streams that cascaded down from the rocks above. For the first time in a long time she was completely at peace. She turned her face up into the water as it rushed down her cheeks. It was oddly warm, and even a little slobbery.

"Oh, Cashew." She opened her eyes and gave the dog a playful shove away from her face. "Did I sleep through your breakfast?" After a wide yawn she sat up in bed. The Yorkshire Terrier pranced across her lap. She ran her hand through the dog's long, silky smooth hair. "Yes, yes, I know. Breakfast." She wiped a hand across her face and considered what awaited her throughout the day. Getting a shop off the ground was a bit harder than she had expected. The great deal she found turned out to be a bit of a construction nightmare. She fed Cashew, then took a shower to wake herself up.

"Remember, Kerri, this was a risk you wanted to take," she said to herself as she rinsed the shampoo out of her shoulder length, dark brown hair and tried to concentrate on the to-do list that carried over from the day before. Get the locks changed, get the shelves up, check the floorboards to see if they needed to be replaced. In her mid-twenties it was a big leap to take, but one visit to the town made her fall in love with it. Between the expansive woods, and the waterfalls nestled in secret places, she just couldn't resist. Since she had a small amount of inheritance from her grandmother, she thought it was worth a try.

Kerri grabbed a muffin for herself, said goodbye to Cashew and then headed out the door. On her drive to the shop she noticed the way the reasonably small town of Cascade Grove woke up. Many people watered their gardens, others walked their dogs. The traffic was light, as it was a bedroom town, but it got quite a few tourists through in the summer months especially on the weekends. Those who worked, left much earlier to get to the city. The few locals who worked in town took their time to open up their shops and restaurants. There was no rush. No one shouted at each other for not driving fast enough, or turning at the wrong time. It was calm compared to the life she was used to. Instead of just a move, or a shift in profession, to her it felt like stepping into an entirely new world.

Kerri parked in front of the shop and stared up at the sign above it. 'L & D Pawnbrokers'. Soon it would read 'Nuts about Nuts'. She'd yet to replace the sign as the new sign was not ready to go up. When she opened the door, she nearly walked right into a man. She gasped and took a step back. It took her a moment to recognize that he wore a uniform from the locksmith company that she had hired to change the locks on the shop.

"How did you get in?" Her cheeks reddened as she realized that was likely a silly question to ask a locksmith.

"I'm sorry if I startled you, ma'am, Natalie let me in."

"Oh, Natalie." Kerri sighed. "I'm sorry, I'm a little scatter-brained this morning." As she walked towards the office she smiled at the handyman who drilled brackets into the wall for shelves. "Morning, Harry. Do you have everything you need?"

"Yes, thanks Kerri. I'll let you know if I have to do another shop for supplies."

Kerri nodded and walked past him towards the office. When she stepped inside her mood was brightened even more by the presence of her employee, and friend, Natalie.

"Morning, Kerri!" She jumped up out of the office chair and grinned at her. Everything about Natalie was perky, from the perky pink bow in her red, curly hair, to the perky red lipstick she wore, to the brightly colored outfits she chose. Maybe that was why Kerri noticed her right away at a community get-together. Kerri saw it as an opportunity to feel out the town, but in the process gained from it a best friend. Although Kerri had friends growing up, she had drifted apart from many of them, and in her twenties she had very few people she could count as close friends. Natalie filled that void as fast as she filled the cup of coffee that she offered Kerri.

"Morning Nat, thank you." She took the coffee and smiled.

"I hope you don't mind that I let the locksmith and Harry in. I just figured the earlier they started the better."

"I don't mind at all. I appreciate it. I am running a little late this morning and it's a relief to know that everything is already started."

"Great, then you're going to be even happier because I made an appointment for you with a reporter from the local newspaper."

"A reporter?" Kerri blew the steam from her coffee. "Why?"

"For advertising of course. He will interview

you about the new shop, when it will be opening, and what customers can expect. It'll be a great way to generate interest and just in time for opening."

"I can't even think about opening yet, when the sign isn't even up." Kerri sat down behind her computer and wiped a hand across her forehead. "I have to admit starting a business is a bit more complicated than I realized."

"Just don't take it too seriously. What's the worst that could happen?" Natalie laughed. Her laughter was punctuated by the sound of shattered glass.

"Oh no!" Kerri jumped up and raced back into the main area of the shop. Natalie followed on her heels. Harry and the locksmith stood over a pile of glass near the door. "What happened?" She looked between the two.

"I'm sorry, a slip of the hand and I broke the window with the hammer. Don't worry, I'll replace it at my cost." Harry wrung his ball cap in his hand. "Sorry for the trouble."

"Harry, don't worry about it. Let me get a broom and dust pan and I'll clean up." She patted his shoulder. "Accidents happen."

"No, don't, I'll take care of it." He walked over to the supply closet. Natalie, quite obviously, watched him go.

"Nat!" Kerri swatted her arm.

"What?" Natalie's eyes widened. "A girl can't appreciate?"

"Back in the office with you." Kerri shooed her away as she laughed. Harry was an attractive man, especially in snug coveralls, but from what Natalie confided in her about past relationships she was the type to fall in love a little too quick. Harry returned with the broom and dust pan to clean up the glass.

"This feels like déjà vu." The locksmith chuckled.

"What do you mean, Graham?" Harry swept the glass into the dustpan.

Kerri walked over to the front counter to

check the supplies she'd accumulated so far. Natalie headed back into the office as the phone rang. As Kerri counted, she overheard their conversation.

"Oh, a few weeks ago when I had to change the locks over at Len's place." He sighed. "Poor man. Anyway, while I was there Delores was cleaning up the glass from the broken window."

"Is that so?" Harry dumped the broken glass into a paper bag.

"Yes, she was quick to clean it up after the police left. She was worried about her little pups getting their paws in the glass when they went outside to do their business."

"The glass was from the window in the broken door?" Harry looked at him. "The one that was broken during the break-in?"

"Yup." Graham tightened the screw on the deadbolt. "All right, Kerri, why don't you try out your new lock?"

"Great." Kerri walked over and took the key

from him. She slid it into the lock and wiggled it a little. Her ears burned, but she hoped the men didn't notice. It was a bit embarrassing for her, but ever since she was a child, if anything sparked her interest, her ears would light up like a flare. It was why she often wore her hair down, but even that was not always enough to hide it. It wasn't the lock that interested her. It was their conversation. The reason why she was able to buy the store for so cheap was because the previous owner was killed. It was a bit morbid, but he was killed at home not in the shop, and she only found out about it after she bought the shop. She probably would have bought it even if she knew about the murder as she couldn't pass up the deal.

"What do you think?" Graham leaned close. "Smooth?"

"Yes, it's perfect." She smiled at him. "I'll need three copies of the key, please. One for me, a spare, and one for Natalie."

"Okay, no problem, I will deliver two more to you this afternoon. Just remember to lock up, this is a small town, but even small towns have their criminals."

"I'll be careful." She was touched by the paternal way he nodded at her. Even though she only just met him, he was interested in looking out for her. It felt so welcoming. Her own youth was spent without much family, as her parents were world travelers, business investors. Her father claimed that was where she got her business bug. She liked to think he was right, as she hoped it would bond them. But he was just as distant as always. She didn't even know in which country her parents were currently.

"Nice to see you, Harry."

"You too, Graham." Harry stared at him for a moment, then returned to the shelves.

Kerri excused herself to go back into the office and found Natalie on the phone.

"Sure, you can come anytime, Steve. Kerri is here."

Kerri cringed. "He's not going to take a

picture is he?" she asked softly and patted at her air-dried hair, and tried to smooth the wrinkles out of her flannel shirt. She'd come to work, to work, not to be photographed.

"Don't worry, Kerri, you look great."

"Natalie!" Kerri gasped as the woman spoke right into the phone.

"Oh oops. Anyway, yes anytime, Steve." She hung up the phone fast and gave Kerri a guilty smile. "I'm sorry, I always get flustered when I talk to him."

"Flustered? Why?" Natalie's cheeks burned bright red. "Natalie?"

"You'll see." She stifled a giggle then jumped up from her office chair. "Off to do some cleaning!"

Chapter Two

Kerri made a few, quick calls to some vendors then consulted her to-do list. One of the major hurdles was a large section of the floor. It hadn't been properly cared for and could lead to a trip and fall. The insurance company insisted it had to be fixed before the store could be opened. She also needed it fixed before the rest of the shelves and the aisles could be set up out front. She was about to go check out the floorboards when her cell phone rang. She pulled it out and checked the number. It wasn't one she recognized. For a moment she hesitated. Did she want to answer and get caught up in some sales spiel, or just let it go to voicemail? On the last ring she decided to answer.

"Hi, this is Kerri."

"Kerri, it's so good to hear your voice."

Her eyes widened. "Grandpa?"

"I hoped you would remember me."

"Of course I do."

"Wonderful. I'm in town."

"What do you mean you're in town?"

"I'm going to stay at the Cascade Grove Hotel. I thought you and I might be able to spend some time together."

"How did you even know I was here?"

"Oh, I have my ways. You don't mind do you?"

Kerri gripped the phone and sat back down in her chair. "No, I don't mind. But this is a busy time right now. I'm trying to open a store, and I'm not sure how much free time I'll have to spend with you."

"Don't worry about that. Just call me when you're free. Maybe for dinner tonight?"

"Uh, sure. Yes, of course. That should be fine. I'll call you later when I know what time. Is everything okay, Grandpa?"

"Yes, fine, I just thought it was time we got to know each other a little better."

Kerri smiled at the thought. All of her memories of her grandfather were adventurous ones. He would sweep in out of the blue and take her skiing, or scuba diving, or to some exotic location. She never knew when he would arrive, and she never knew when he would leave. But he was always a lot of fun.

"That sounds great. I'm looking forward to it."

"Me too, Kerri."

As she hung up the phone she couldn't help but wonder how he had hunted her down, and why. No matter the reason she had to focus on getting the floors done. As she stepped out of the office Natalie walked past her towards the office.

"I'm going to confirm the deliveries for tomorrow."

"Great. Make sure they know that all deliveries are to go to the back door. I'm not sure what state the floors out here will be in tomorrow."

"Will do."

Kerri spent the next few hours going over the floorboards with the hope that she would be able to forego replacing the planks. However, it didn't take long for her to realize that the scuffed, worn, and sometimes burnt surface of the wood wasn't going to refinish well. She sighed and stood up. That would be another unexpected expense. After a brief freak out in her mind, she took a deep breath and walked over to the supply closet. She rummaged around for a moment, then found what she hoped to.

"Kerri, what are you doing with that crowbar?" Harry crossed his arms as she walked past him towards one of the floorboards behind the front counter.

"I just want to see how much of this I can do myself." She shoved the edge of the bar under the floorboard.

"You don't need to, I can do it." Harry reached for the crowbar.

"No, really, I can do it. In fact, you should probably get going. The shelves look great, but I'm going to need you here bright and early tomorrow to finish setting up the shelves in the back, and then once the floors are done you can set up the aisles and some more shelving out the front."

"Okay, but be careful with that. It can easily slip."

"Thanks, I will."

She pried up a few more floorboards, then rested for a moment.

"Kerri, I'm going to step out to see if I can arrange a grand opening banner for cheap with a friend of mine at the photo shop. Is that okay?" Natalie eyed the floor. "What in the world are you doing?"

"Trying to cut corners just like you." Kerri winked at her. "That banner sounds great. Thanks, Nat."

"Do you want some help?" Natalie smoothed down her pink, frilled skirt. "I can see if there's another crowbar."

"No, it's okay really. I'm not going to do much

today. I just wanted to get a feel for how much needs to be done."

"All right, take it easy, Boss, I'll be back."

Kerri rolled her eyes at the title and laughed as she picked up the crowbar again. She pulled up a few more boards then slid the crowbar under another.

"Hello?"

The voice from the doorway coincided with the dig of the crowbar, which flipped the already loose floorboard high into the air.

"Watch out!" She jumped back as the floorboard soared over the counter. The man in the entrance of the shop jumped back as well. The floorboard clattered right in front of his feet.

"That was close." He winced.

"I'm so sorry!" She rushed around the counter towards him, but the moment she laid eyes on him she froze. His black wavy hair, sharp blue eyes, and broad shoulders caused her heart to skip a beat. He might have been the most handsome man she'd ever set eyes on, and there she was covered in sweat, and wrinkled clothes.

"It's all right, I'm sure that you didn't mean to fling that board at me. Did you?" He looked into her eyes.

"No, of course I didn't. I didn't expect anyone to be here, and the board was much looser than I expected."

"I see, well, I don't quite see, but Natalie told me I could come by anytime. So I'm here." He cleared his throat. "I'm sorry I haven't even introduced myself. I'm Steve Newis." He offered her his hand. She started to raise hers, until she realized that she still had the crowbar clutched in it. She laughed and dropped it to the floor. It clattered louder than she expected.

"Kerri Gale." She took his hand, only to cringe at the thought of just how sweaty hers was. She pulled it back and wiped it on her jeans. "I'm sorry, I got caught up in work and forgot that you were even coming."

"Don't apologize, I can see that you have a lot

on your shoulders here. Do you have a partner?"

"Oh no, I'm chronically single."

He laughed, his eyes crinkled at the edges when he did. "I meant, do you have a partner in the business."

Her cheeks flamed. "No, it's just me."

"That's a big undertaking, especially at your age."

"Twenty-four? I don't think that's too big of a step."

"When I was twenty-four, I was still trying to figure out what to do with my life." He shrugged and slipped his hands into his pockets.

"That couldn't be too long ago."

"No, not too long, just three years. A lot changed in those years though."

"Like what?" She studied him.

"Hey, I thought I was here to ask the questions." He grinned.

"I'm sorry, it's my nature to be inquisitive.

People tell me all the time I come on a little too strong."

"You won't hear that from me. It's refreshing to meet someone who has an honest interest. Most people just want to gloss over the surface of things without any real connection."

"You've noticed that, too?" She shook her head. "I don't understand chit-chat."

"Well then, let's cut to the interview. I don't want to interfere with your progress here."

"Sure. My office?" She gestured to the door.

"Okay, lead the way."

Once they were settled in the office, she regretted the invitation. When she was in the room with Natalie it didn't feel tiny, but now that she sat across from Steve it seemed there wasn't enough space between them. Steve shifted in his chair and pulled a small notepad out of his pocket along with a short pencil. Right away she was intrigued by the fact that he didn't use a computer or tablet like most reporters did.

"So, tell me a little bit about why you decided to move here. I know that you're not a local."

"Oh, you've done your research?" She smiled.

"No, it's just that I know every local, and you're not one of them." He tapped his pencil against the pad of paper. "I also might have done just a little research."

"Just a little? Honestly, I visited here once and fell in love with the place. When I had an opportunity to make a move, I decided to move here."

"It seems like a big leap to make. Are you always so impulsive?" His eyes narrowed some as he gazed into her eyes.

"I don't know if I'd call it impulsive. This town is a great place to open a business, which is something I always knew I wanted to do."

"So, you have a passion for nuts?"

She laughed. "Not just nuts. When I was younger my parents traveled a lot. My favorite part of any trip was visiting the gourmet shops.

Every place had something unique. It was a new flavor, new texture, new packaging. I want to bring that joy to other people. I know many people don't have the opportunity to travel the world, so my goal is to bring the world to one small shop in one small town. I source locally and also import a variety of nuts, fruits, unique foods, and small gifts."

He leaned forward. "It must have been a little lonely to always be on the go like that."

"What does that have to do with the shop?" She tilted her head to the side.

"It's just a question." He shrugged. "Off the record."

"I was very lucky to get to see so much of the world."

"And what about your family? Were you close?"

"I think these questions are getting a little personal."

"Like I said, off the record. I'm a little

inquisitive myself. But please forgive me if I've crossed a line. I just find your move here to be very interesting."

"Well, it won't be much of a move if I don't get the shop up and on its feet fast. So, if you don't have any more questions for the article…"

"I'm sorry, I really didn't mean to upset you."

She smiled. "You didn't. It's just I really do need to get back to work."

"Maybe I could come by tomorrow to snap some pictures of the shop for the article?"

"Yes, that would be great." Kerri tried not to show how flustered she was. Steve's questions surprised her, as they touched on topics that she was not very comfortable talking about. "I'll walk you out. I want to get you some samples, so that you can write a glowing review."

"I never turn down samples." He grinned as he leaned against the front counter. She tried not to notice the dimples in his cheeks. Now she understood what Natalie meant when she spoke about Steve. As she rounded the counter she stumbled on some of the floorboards that she had pried up. Steve caught her by the elbow before she could fall.

"Are you okay?"

"Yes, thanks." She stared down into one of the open spaces beneath the floorboards. Her heart skipped a beat as she looked closer. "What is that?"

"Something tucked away?" He peered at it as well as she crouched down beside the opening. Inside, she could see three bundled stacks of money. Even though she saw it clearly, she still doubted her own eyes. How could there be that much money hidden in the floor? She picked up one stack and ran her fingertips along the paper money band that held it together.

"Where did this come from?"

"I better call the police." Steve fished his phone out of his pocket.

"The police? Why?" She dropped the stack of

money back into the hole.

"They were never able to pin down a motive behind Len's murder, the best they could come up with was a robbery gone wrong. It's one of the very few unsolved crimes around here. This money might be that motive."

"But the money is still there? Obviously they didn't get it."

"All the more reason to report it to the police." He began to call them. Her mind spun as she listened to him give the description of what they had found and where. Would she be in trouble? He hung up the phone and looked into her eyes.

"It's okay, the police will handle everything."

"Are you sure? What if they think I knew it was here?"

"Why would they think that?" He shrugged. "You might have found evidence in Len's murder. Maybe it could even lead to the murder being solved."

"I hope so. It would be nice if there was some

justice for his murder."

"I think so, too. Len wasn't the most well-liked guy around here, but he wasn't a bad guy either. He was just trying to make a living."

"Well, if that's his money, then it looks like he might have been doing more than that. Do you think he was involved in something illegal?" She brushed her hair down over her ears to hide the heat that she felt rush into them. A genuine mystery made her senses flutter with interest.

"I can't say for sure. But maybe this will help us find out."

A siren blared outside the shop. Kerri looked from the door, to Steve. "I hate talking to police."

"Don't worry about that. I can talk to Meyers with you."

"Meyers?"

A large man with a wide-brimmed hat walked into the shop. He adjusted it, and looked at the two of them.

"Steve, did you call something in?"

"Yes, I did." He tilted his head towards Kerri. "This is Kerri, the new owner. When she pulled up some floorboards she found some money hidden underneath."

"And you decided to turn it in?" He raised an eyebrow.

"It's not mine." Kerri shrugged. "If it's part of something illegal I want nothing to do with it."

"That's a lot of money." He studied her for a moment.

"It is," Kerri said. "It must belong to Len's family now."

"There's only his wife, Delores, and his brother, Chris. No one has heard from him since shortly after Len's death."

"Well, they should have it," Kerri said.

"I'll take this to be logged in as evidence in the case," he said as he started bagging up the money. "However, I'm not sure how much it will do for the investigation. After some time it will be released to the family, if it is found to be legal."

"Do you think it might have been the reason that Len's place was broken into and he was killed?" Steve pulled out his notepad.

"Off the record, Steve, you know better than that."

"All right." He tucked the notepad back in his pocket.

"I'm not sure what to think. If this was the motive, then why did someone break into Len's house, why not here?" Detective Meyers asked.

"Maybe, they thought Len had it hidden in the house." Kerri frowned. "I mean, it took prying up several floorboards to find it. He hid it well."

"Yes, he did. But running a legitimate pawn shop doesn't get you this kind of money. If this did belong to Len, then he was up to something that he shouldn't have been," Detective Meyers said.

"Like what?" Kerri stepped closer. "Do you think it's anything I need to worry about?"

"Honestly, maybe drugs. Maybe money laundering. It's hard to say without a little more investigating. However, with Len dead, it will be difficult to get to the bottom of it. I'll make the best effort I can though. Oh, and Kerri, if you find anything else, be sure to report it to us as soon as possible. Okay?"

"Sure." She nodded. "I'm going to try to finish prying up most of the floorboards today, so I'll let you know."

"Great. And Steve, I'm sure I don't have to remind you that I don't want to see anything about this until the chief authorizes the release of information."

"Meyers, be reasonable. I was here when the money was discovered. I have every right to release that information."

"You want to worry about your rights, or you want to worry about your freedom?" He locked eyes with Steve. "Chief Higgins will find a way to put you behind bars if you even think about publishing anything before he approves it."

"That doesn't sound legal." Kerri scrunched up her nose. "What about freedom of information?"

"Young lady, you're new to this town, but there are a few things you'll learn fast. What Chief Higgins says goes, and because of that, this is one of the safest towns to live in. He's a fair man, when he feels it's safe he will give Steve the go-ahead to publish. Isn't that right, Steve?" Detective Meyers tipped his hat.

"Yes, but you know this news will travel fast, I don't want to be the last one to publish it."

"It's your risk to take." He nodded to Kerri, then turned and walked out of the shop.

"That was quite strange. I don't think any chief-of-police should have that much influence on a town." She crossed her arms and turned to look at Steve. "Is this really how it is here?"

"It is. Scare tactics don't work on me. I will be publishing what I know. You don't mind, do you?"

"If it's news, it's news. It's not like the whole town won't hear about it either way."

"Exactly. So, call me first if you find anything

else, okay?"

"Okay." She walked him to the door. She had the sense that she should be careful just who she trusted in the town. "Good luck with your story."

"Thanks." The door swung shut behind him. Kerri leaned back against the door and stared at the torn up floor. It was an interesting surprise to find the money. Even though it stirred up a little stress about whether it would affect the store's reputation, she was curious about whether it would lead to a murder being solved. In fact, as she pried up the rest of the boards in the shop area that needed replacing, she became more and more determined to discover what might have really happened to Len. A few hours later, the floors were done, and her arms ached from the effort, but she didn't find a trace of evidence. It occurred to her that maybe the money had nothing to do with Len after all. Maybe he didn't even know it was there. She wiped her brow and glanced at her watch. It was late, and Cashew had to be starving. She put the tools away and locked up.

Chapter Three

When Kerri pulled into the driveway of her house it was almost dark. Her body ached as she walked towards the door. She slid the key into the lock, then realized the door was already unlocked. She froze. Tension rippled through her chest. How could it be unlocked? She was always careful about things like that. She was sure she hadn't left it unlocked. Inside she heard movement. It didn't sound like Cashew. It sounded like someone much larger. Could it be related to the money that she had found? She held her breath and turned the door knob. When she pushed open the door she saw a man hunched over and digging through her front closet.

"I'm calling the police right now!" She grabbed her phone from her purse. He spun around to face her with wide eyes.

"Now, don't do that, it will ruin the surprise." He grinned.

"Grandpa!" She dropped her phone. "What are you doing sneaking around?"

He laughed as he picked up her phone for her. "I wanted to surprise you. When you didn't call me about dinner, I thought I'd come over here before I checked into the hotel to make it for you."

"But how did you get in?"

"Oh, your old grandfather still has a few tricks up his sleeve. Anyway, did you know that your poor little dog was starving?"

"She doesn't eat until I get home." She tucked her phone back into her pocket, still dazed by his presence. "I'm sorry about dinner, I forgot. I got caught up in something at work."

"Yes, you found a bunch of money, didn't you?"

She stared at him. "How would you know about that?"

"Tricks." He winked at her and pointed to his sleeve. "Anyway, let's not talk about that now. Let's have a nice dinner together, okay? I made chicken stir-fry."

"You did?" She took a deep breath and smiled. "Wow, that smells great."

"It wasn't easy, you didn't have much in your fridge."

"I know, I've been a little too busy for grocery shopping."

"Tsk. You have to nourish yourself first or you will never get anywhere in life. Let's eat." He walked towards the kitchen as if he was inviting her into his home. Kerri followed after him with some hesitation. What made him think it was okay to just show up in her home? Didn't he think that she had a right to privacy? Then again, she didn't know all that much about her grandfather, other than the fun excursions he would take her on, they didn't spend a lot of time together. When she stepped into the kitchen she saw the table already set with lit candles.

"Wow, you didn't have to go to all of this trouble."

"It's no trouble to get to spend an evening with my favorite granddaughter."

"Only granddaughter." She grinned.

"Still my favorite." He filled her plate from the pan, then filled his as well. "I was also quite disappointed to see that you have no wine in this house."

"I'm not much of a drinker."

"Well, neither am I, but it's not dinner without a glass of wine, is it?"

She shrugged. "There should be some orange juice in there."

"It will have to do. But only if we drink it in these." He set two wine glasses on the table and poured orange juice into them. "A toast, to us." He held up the wine glass. Despite the ache in her arms from tearing up the floors, and the questions that swirled in her mind about her grandfather's presence, she raised her glass and touched it to his. Although he had aged and his black hair was now speckled with gray, he still had the same strong presence with his athletic body and towering frame at almost six feet tall. As they both took a sip of the orange juice she realized how much she enjoyed having him there. It had been so long since she had a family member to confide in.

"I'm glad you came to visit, Grandpa. I'm so overwhelmed right now with opening the shop, and then unexpectedly coming across possible evidence in a murder."

"A murder?" He looked up at her with surprise. "Who was killed?"

"The previous owner of the shop. He ran a pawn shop. There was a break-in at his home and he was killed."

"And they haven't caught the killer?"

"No. As far as I can tell things have been pretty cold, until I found the money today. How did you hear about that?"

"I keep an ear to the police chatter wherever I am."

"Why?" She raised an eyebrow.

"Eat your stir-fry." He pointed to her plate. "And no skipping the carrots."

"I eat carrots now, Grandpa." She laughed, then took a bite and complimented the taste. After a few seconds of silence, she looked at him again. "Why do you listen to the police chatter?"

"That's more like after-dinner talk."

"Okay." Kerri raised an eyebrow. Her grandfather had always been a little mysterious, but this was downright evasive. "I can't believe you found me so easily. I've only been here for a couple of weeks."

"I know, I always know where you are. It's my job to keep track of you, Kerri."

"I don't need anyone to keep track of me." Kerri laughed. "I've managed up until now."

"I know that." He set down his fork and met her eyes with his own green eyes that were just slightly darker than hers. They were the same shade as her father's eyes. "I know that you're used to taking care of yourself, and you didn't have your mother or father around much. But don't think for a second that you weren't looked out for. We always made sure that you were safe, in more ways than you realize."

Kerri finished her bite of food and set down her fork as well. "Then tell me those ways. Why are you really here, Grandpa? What's the visit for?"

"It's not a visit. I'm here to stay. I just have to find a place to settle in."

"Wait, you're moving here?"

"Yes." He smiled. "You don't mind do you?"

"No, I don't mind. I'm just a little surprised. I don't think I've ever even known your address."

"It's time for me to put down roots, Kerri. I want those roots to be near family. I want to be the grandfather to you that I never had a chance to be. Is that something that you would like?"

"Sure. I'd love the chance to get to know you better. It's just a busy time for me right now."

"I can help you with that. I can help in the shop, help out with Cashew here." He tossed the small dog a sliver of chicken.

"Grandpa, she doesn't get table food."

"Poor pup." He shook his head. "Imagine going through life with nothing but dog food?"

"She's a dog, so it's probably gourmet to her."

"Maybe. You're so interesting to me, Kerri."

"I am?" She smiled. "I don't know why."

"Your father, your mother, me, we're all roamers. You seem to have a talent for knowing what you want and how to get it."

"Maybe, but the shop isn't open yet, and with this delay I'm not sure when it will be."

"Why is there a delay?"

"Well, if the police decide they need to investigate the shop then I will have to put off the grand opening."

"There's a simple solution for that."

"There is?" She shook her head. "What?"

"Let's solve the murder. Then the issue will be out of your hair, and you'll make quite a reputation for yourself in your new home."

"Sure, but it's not that simple."

"Why not? You've got a great mind for detail. You always have. You used to solve all of my little quizzes."

"Quizzes?" She grinned. "You mean those riddles and brain teasers?"

"To you, they were games, but to me it was training."

"I have no idea what you're talking about, Grandpa."

"You will, in time. Finish your food before it gets cold."

Kerri shook her head but continued to eat. It was rather nice to have family around, but she suspected that her grandfather had some underlying purpose for his presence. It wasn't as if they spent holidays together. For him to just pop in out of the blue was strange enough, but for him to declare he wasn't leaving, was almost impossible to believe. After dinner she began to wash the dishes. However, her focus was on what her grandfather would have to say, and the idea that they could solve the murder. Why not? The police didn't seem to have a clue to go on. What could it hurt if she and her grandfather looked into it?

"Grandpa, I'm going to take Cashew for a walk. Do you want to join us?"

"Sure, just give me a few minutes. I need to make a call."

"Okay, we'll meet you outside." She snapped a leash onto Cashew's collar and led her out through the front door. Cashew bounced more than she walked, she was so excited to be outside. Kerri wished she could keep her with her at the shop. She'd asked Natalie to stop by to walk her in the middle of the day, but she missed her time with the pup.

As Kerri waited for her grandfather, she remembered there were nuts to unload from her trunk. She decided to bring them home so she could try out some recipes. She popped the trunk and grabbed a couple of boxes to take inside. However, with Cashew so excited, she got her leash tangled around Kerri's feet. Kerri stumbled and one of the boxes slid out of her hands. It hit the ground hard and a few bags of nuts scattered. She sighed and retrieved the bags then tucked them back into the box. She opened the back door to stow them inside. When she did, she heard her grandfather's voice.

"No, she doesn't suspect anything. It surprises me. She's always been such a clever girl, but I guess she's clueless when it comes to this."

Kerri's mouth dropped open. Was he talking about her? She lingered just inside the door and continued to listen.

"It is the right time, there is no other time. She deserves to know the truth. It's hard, I know, but she's going to have to be told some time, before she figures it out on her own." He paused. Cashew whimpered.

"I'll let you know. Yes, everything is in place."

Kerri hurried Cashew away from the back door. She knew that if her grandfather caught her listening in, there would be even more to explain. Her heart raced as she wondered what he meant. Was it a coincidence that he showed up now? Before she could figure anything out he walked around from the front.

"There you are, Kerri! I was looking for you."

"Sorry, I had some nuts to unload from my car." She avoided looking him in the eye.

Cashew jumped up and down and nosed his ankle. "It looks like Cashew is ready for her walk." He paused and glanced towards the woods. "Looks like that squirrel is ready for his lunch."

Kerri looked in the direction he pointed just in time to see a squirrel with his tiny paws grasping a large bag of nuts.

"What are you doing?" Kerri put her hands on her hips. "That bag is way too big for one squirrel."

The squirrel dropped the bag of nuts, but it

broke open from his clawing. His fluffy tail shot straight up as he attacked the nuts that scattered across the ground.

"That squirrel is getting a feast." Her grandfather grinned as he watched.

"Yes, on gourmet nuts!" Kerri laughed. "I'm sure he's never had a nut quite like that before."

Cashew crouched down low and watched the squirrel, too. But instead of barking or lunging, Cashew nudged one of the lost nuts in the squirrel's direction. The squirrel stopped and stared.

"Would you look at that?"

"Be nice, Cashew." Kerri crouched down beside the dog. The squirrel inched close enough to grab the nut, then bolted for a nearby tree with his cheeks stuffed. Kerri noticed that he had a streak of black down his back. She thought that was unusual for a squirrel.

"I'm so glad I chose this house. I love being so close to the woods."

"It's a very nice place. You made a good choice." As they began to walk along the road Kerri couldn't stop thinking about what he'd said on the phone.

"So, is this 'after-dinner' enough for some answers?"

"You have such a keen mind."

"Flattery will get you nowhere, Grandpa. Why so many secrets?"

"Honestly, it's habit I guess. Secrets have always been a necessary part of my life."

"But why? That's what I don't understand. What is there to be so secretive about?"

"Kerri, I want you to trust me."

"You're my grandfather."

"Not just because I'm your grandfather, but because you know that you can trust me. No matter what."

"Okay." She let Cashew sniff around and focused on her grandfather. "Then tell me the truth. Honesty is the best way to gain trust."

"Perhaps. But I'm afraid it might be a little late for that."

"Are you in some kind of trouble, Grandpa? Did you come here to hide out?"

He smiled and shook his head. "No. I'm not hiding out. I'm retiring."

"But you've been retired for some time."

"Retired from my job as a museum curator. Yes, of course."

"I don't understand." She frowned.

"You're tired. I'm tired. Why don't we talk about this in the morning? I should get to the hotel before it gets too late."

"Wait, there's no reason for you to stay in a hotel. I have an extra room here. It will give us a chance to spend some time together. If you want to, that is."

"I'd be honored. Thank you for the invitation. Are you sure it wouldn't be too much of an inconvenience."

"No, it's fine with me. It'll be nice to have

some company."

When they returned to the house Kerri thought about asking more questions, but her grandfather excused himself to bed in the guest room before she could. Her mind swirled with a mixture of apprehension and excitement. All of her life something had seemed a little off. Maybe, finally, her grandfather would be able to explain that.

Chapter Four

Early the next morning Kerri arrived at the shop, more determined than ever to get everything into place. When she left the house, her grandfather was still asleep so she decided not to wake him. She would have time to grill him later, once the floors were done. When she walked up to the door she was surprised to find that Harry waited outside for her.

"What are you doing here so early?" She smiled at him.

"I knew you'd need help with the floors. I'd like to help you out with them, no extra charge."

"No extra charge?" She raised an eyebrow. "Why is that?"

"I heard what you found yesterday. Len was a friend of mine. If there's anything else that can be done that might help solve his murder, I want to figure out what it is."

She looked at him for a long moment. "Do you

have any idea who did it?"

"I have my theories." He narrowed his eyes. "Why?"

"I'm just curious."

"Be mighty careful what you stick your nose into. Around here there are many skeletons to uncover."

"Really? It seems like such a quiet, little town."

"Quiet and little yes, but scandals are something that happen everywhere you go. It's not easy to explain the 'why' or the 'how' when everyone with deep pockets wants it kept quiet."

"Interesting." She unlocked the front door and led him inside. "I finished tearing up the floorboards yesterday. Now, we can concentrate on putting in the new wood."

"Great. Did it get delivered?"

"It should be out back. I have a delivery confirmation email."

"I'll check on it." He headed towards the back

door of the shop. Kerri took a moment to watch him go. She wondered if he was as honest as he appeared to be. With the discovery of the money under the floorboards, then her grandfather showing up, and now the handyman offering to work for free she felt as if she'd stepped into a strange new dimension. What happened to the simple and boring life she left behind? As she started to sort through the paperwork she had to complete for the deliveries she would receive that day, her cell phone rang. She noticed it was Natalie.

"Hi, Nat. I thought you were starting later today?"

"I am, but I was hoping that we could meet for breakfast. I want to discuss something with you."

"Okay, sure." She glanced at her watch. "I can get away for a little bit."

"There's a nice breakfast spot on Vincent Street, Cascade Café. I'll meet you there, okay?"

"I'll be there." She hung up the phone and poked her head into the back of the shop. Harry was hauling the wood from the delivery inside.

"Harry, I'm going to step out. You don't have to work on this if you don't want to. But if you do, feel free to get started. And no matter what you say, I will be paying you for it."

He smiled. "If that's what you want, it's fine with me."

"Great. I should be back in about an hour."

"Maybe I'll be done by then." He winked at her.

"If you are, I'll pay you double." She laughed as she walked out of the shop. A breakfast with Natalie was exactly what she needed. Her friend had a way of clearing her mind, no matter how mixed up her thoughts were.

When she arrived at the café Natalie was already seated inside. Kerri joined her at the table and smiled.

"Good morning."

"Good morning to you." Natalie yawned.

"You don't seem very awake."

"I've already ordered coffee."

"Is something up?" Kerri studied her friend.

"I had a hard time sleeping last night. Ever since you found that money all I can think about is Len, and what really happened to him."

"I know, it was disturbing to me, too. But you knew him, didn't you?"

"Just in passing. He wasn't the type of person that I associated with. But, that's not what has me concerned."

"Then what is it?" Kerri reached out and touched her hand. "I'm here, you can tell me anything."

"That means a lot, because when I tell you this I'm pretty sure that you're going to think I'm crazy."

"I already think that, sweetie." She patted her hand.

"Kerri! I'm serious."

"I'm sorry." Kerri grinned. "But trust me, there's nothing that you could tell me that would change my high opinion of you."

"I hope so." Natalie bit into her bottom lip for a moment, then leaned close. When she spoke, it was in a whisper. "What if Len is the one who broke the window?"

"What? In his house?"

"No. In the shop. Remember?"

"Yesterday morning?"

"Yes."

"How could he possibly do that?" She paused. "Oh."

"See? That's the look. The, 'Natalie, you're so crazy look'."

"It's not that look. I'm just surprised. I didn't know you believe in ghosts."

"I don't, I mean. I don't believe in them, but I don't not believe in them either."

"I'm confused."

"It's like this. I have no idea what happens when somebody dies. But I'm pretty sure that if I was murdered, I'd try to find a way to come back and point out my murderer. So, is it really far-fetched to believe that Len might have a hand in the window breaking and the money being found?"

Kerri sat back in her chair. She didn't want to offend her friend, the only real friend she'd made since moving in, but she also didn't have much belief in the paranormal.

"It's something to consider. I guess it doesn't really change things either way. Whether it's Len's spirit reaching out to us or not, I am determined to try and figure out what happened to him."

"You are?" Natalie smiled. "That's great. I want to help. How can we figure it out?"

"That part I'm not sure about. I thought maybe we could involve Steve."

"Oh yes, anything that involves Steve is fine with me." Natalie smiled.

"You could have warned me about how handsome he is."

"I didn't want you to be nervous."

"Sure. Or you just wanted him to see me all wrinkled and sweaty."

Natalie burst out laughing and startled the waitress who brought over two cups of coffee. "Sorry, cream please." Once the coffee was settled and the orders were placed, Natalie looked across the table at Kerri. "Yes, I will admit that Steve is drop-dead gorgeous, but you have nothing to worry about. I admire him from afar, but I would never throw my hat into that ring."

"Why not?" Kerri did her best to pretend the question was casual.

"Because I want more than a pretty face. I want a man I can settle down with, have babies with, watch television with. Steve, he's the adventurous type. The kind that would make me climb a mountain, or I don't know, sign up for a triathlon or something. Not my speed." She shook her head. "I like, cozy on the couch with a movie, not a reporter that will jump on a grenade for a story."

"You seem to know him pretty well."

"We went to school together, and trust me he hasn't changed much. He was always getting himself into some kind of trouble. That's just too much work for me." She laughed and took a sip of her coffee. Kerri laughed as well, but only to cover the heat in her ears. There it was, interest, whether she liked it or not. Adventurous was just what she craved in her life. She decided to change the subject before her ears made it to a shade of purple.

"I had my own little surprise last night. My grandfather is in town, and he just popped into my house to make me dinner."

"Without asking?"

"He broke in." She smiled at the waitress as she delivered their food.

"Wait, your grandfather broke into your house? What kind of grandfather does that?"

"George. That's what kind. He's pretty unique."

"I'd say so. My grandfather just asks me when I'm finding a husband, every single time I see him." She rolled her eyes. "So, how long is he staying?"

"That's the other strange thing. He's not visiting. He's here to stay."

"He's moving in with you?"

Kerri's heart stopped. She hadn't even considered that. But was that her grandfather's intention? She didn't think she'd be able to turn him away if it was. Was it right to tell a family member that she preferred to live alone?

"Uh, we haven't really talked about that. I asked him to stay with me instead of at the hotel, but we didn't discuss whether it would be permanent."

"It all seems odd. Do you think he might be a little senile?"

Kerri almost choked on her coffee. "No, absolutely not. He's the most astute man I've ever known."

"Tell me a little about him. What does he do for a living? What does he like?"

Kerri frowned and pushed her eggs around on her plate. "He worked as a curator for a museum. However, I never got to actually visit the museum. Whenever I saw him he had the most fantastic stories, and the most unique finds. Ancient statues, toys from every country. Honestly, I don't know much more than that about him. I didn't know him very well growing up. I'd see him now and then, but not very often. However, every time I did, it was an adventure. He took me zip-lining, to visit a rain forest, exotic things like that."

"Wow, that does sound like a lot of fun. Well, what does your dad say about him?"

Kerri shrugged. "We don't really talk."

"Your mom?" Natalie stared across the table at her.

"She is quite secretive. We've never been very close, she's always traveling with my dad."

"Oh, Kerri, I'm sorry. Didn't you have anyone

when you were growing up?"

"I had my grandmother, my mother's mother, when I was young, before she passed away. I had lots of adventures, and lots of memories, and a great education. So, in many ways I've had more than most."

"Maybe. I really cherish being close to my family. I always know that I have someone that I can turn to. That makes me feel safe."

"I'm sure it does." Kerri smiled warmly. "I think that's great."

"You have me now, Kerri. I mean it. You can always turn to me for anything that you need."

"Thanks, Nat. I appreciate that."

"But there is one little thing, if the shop is haunted, I'm going to have to quit. Okay?"

"What?" Kerri's eyes widened.

"I can't spend every day dealing with a ghost. I'd be terrified."

"I think you're getting a little ahead of yourself, Natalie. I promise there's no ghost."

"If you say so."

"I'll tell you what, if it turns out the place is haunted, you can work from home, doing ordering and other administration stuff. How does that sound?"

"I think I could handle that." Natalie nodded.

"Harry's back at the shop working on the floors for me. We should bring him back something to eat." She signaled the waitress. "Any idea what he might like?"

"Pancakes and sausage are a sure bet," Natalie said. When the waitress walked over Kerri ordered the meal to go and handed her the money to cover the bill.

"Kerri, I invited you, you should let me pay."

"Please, it's just a little thing I can do for you. Is it too big of an issue?"

"No, but you can't do this every time."

"Hmm, last person that told me what to do..." She laughed. "I can't remember the last person who told me what to do, actually."

"That's funny. I can't remember the last time I made a decision all on my own. Well, not until I came to work for you. Kerri, I think the store is going to be a great success."

"I hope so. I know I will enjoy running it."

The waitress returned with a receipt and the extra meal.

"Thanks for breakfast, Kerri." Natalie smiled. Kerri's heart filled with warmth for the woman across the table from her. Though they'd only known each other for a short time, Natalie had offered her loyalty and friendship without the slightest hesitation. That was something that Kerri treasured.

As they left for the store together, Natalie pointed out different areas of the town and rattled off wild memories.

"That's where Shawn Thomson got his head stuck, see, in the bike rack?" She laughed. "He got stuck right after school because he was fooling around. Well, the school called his mother, and his mother showed up. She tried to get him out, but she couldn't. So she told him he had to stay there. She let him sit there for hours before the fire chief insisted on getting him free."

"How horrible! Why would his mother do that to him?"

"Shawn had a habit of getting himself stuck places and he still did even after the incident. I think she thought she was teaching him a lesson." Natalie shrugged. "Who knows?"

"That's quite a lesson."

"Yes, it was. Funny though." Natalie grinned.

"Yes, it is pretty funny." Kerri laughed.

Chapter Five

When Kerri and Natalie returned to the shop Kerri juggled the breakfast to her other hand so that she could open the door.

"Harry?" She heard the buzz of a sander and assumed that he couldn't hear her. "Harry! Take a break, we brought you breakfast!"

"I'll just pop in the office to check the messages." Natalie walked past her towards the office door. Kerri followed the sound of the sander into the back room. With a smile she held the take-out box in front of her. However, the box tumbled to the floor when her hands grew too numb to hold it. On the floor beside the sander was Harry. She must have screamed. Her chest ached, her eyes watered, and Natalie came running to her side. She heard Natalie's scream, but she never heard her own. She dropped down to her knees to check for a pulse. Once she determined that Harry didn't have one she scrambled for her phone to call for help.

"They're on their way, Kerri. I already called. Poor Harry, oh poor Harry," Natalie gasped and wrung her hands. Kerri could barely hear her over the sander. Numbly she switched it to off. The silence that filled the small space struck her hard in the gut. Harry's glassy eyes stared up at her. She tried not to look at the sander cord around his neck. Could it have been some kind of tragic accident? Was it really possible to get an electrical cord tangled around your own neck? Within minutes the back room was filled with police officers, Detective Meyers, and of course, Steve. He walked right over to Kerri and Natalie.

"Let's get you two out of here and into some fresh air, hmm?" He spoke to both of them, but his eyes fixated on Kerri, probably because she looked so shocked. Steve led them out through the back door. In the back of her mind she noted that a few of the deliveries had been made.

"How did this happen?" Kerri stared at the back door. "I wasn't gone very long."

"Just try to take a deep breath, Kerri. You're

probably in shock," Steve said.

"Was it an accident, do you think, Steve?" Natalie grabbed Kerri's hand and held it tight.

"No, that was no accident. Someone did this to Harry, and until the police make an arrest I think you should stay away from the shop. Both of you."

"I can't do that, the grand opening and..."

"Kerri, your shop is now a crime scene. You're going to have to wait for the police to complete their investigation before they'll allow you to open it."

Tears bit at her eyes. They weren't tears for the shop, but tears for the man who had made such a kind effort to help her.

"He was only here because he wanted to help me with the floors. That's all he wanted. If I'd said no, if I hadn't gone to breakfast, maybe he'd still be alive."

"You can't think like that, Kerri." Natalie squeezed her hand. "This isn't your fault. There's nothing that you could have done."

"Natalie's right. Whoever did this, came after Harry. I don't think it has anything to do with your store. But to be on the safe side, you should have someone stay at the house with you."

"My grandfather, he's there with me."

"Oh? I didn't realize you had family here," Steve said.

"I didn't, he just arrived." She sighed and shook her head. "This is all too much. It doesn't make any sense. Len was killed, and now Harry."

"It might not be related."

"But it might be. Can you tell me anything about Len's death? Do you think that they could be related?"

Steve gritted his teeth and looked away. "I'm not sure you want to get in the middle of that."

"I could not be any more in the middle of it. Could I?" She stared at him. "Harry's dead. Len's dead. Something isn't right here."

"I'm telling you, it's Len, getting his revenge.

I bet Harry had something to do with his murder. Maybe he broke into Len's house." Natalie narrowed her eyes. "It makes sense, doesn't it?"

"No." Steve locked eyes with her. "There was nothing spiritual about the way that cord was wrapped around Harry's neck. Someone with flesh and muscle murdered him."

"Okay, maybe you're right." Natalie shrugged. "But who?"

"Yes, who." Kerri crossed her arms as she looked at Steve. "I know that you know more about Len's death than you're saying. Harry mentioned he had his suspicions, but he never told me who or why."

"Look, Len made a few enemies in town, but none that I thought would kill him. The only theory I ever had, which I had no evidence to back up, was that perhaps Len and Chris had some falling out."

"His brother?" Natalie's eyes widened. "But they were always so close."

"You're right. But things can change when you mix family with business. Chris became Len's partner not long before Len was killed. They were going to change the name to 'L & C Pawnbrokers'."

"How do you know that?" Kerri glanced over her shoulder at the crowd that began gathering around the shop. The lights and sirens were enough to get the attention of most.

"Because I did some research after Len was killed. I never thought the case was handled properly. The investigation was too fast, and it led to nothing. I thought I'd take a stab at it. All I found was that Len and Chris were tangled up financially. Maybe that's a motive for murder."

"If things went wrong. Did they?" Kerri asked.

"I don't know." Steve frowned. "I hit a roadblock. I couldn't find any reason for the two to be fighting. So, I just assumed that my hunch was wrong. Chris disappeared after Len's death, and Len's wife put the shop up for sale. I have no idea how Harry would be caught up in all of it. But now I'm not so sure my hunch was wrong."

"What's changed your mind?"

"I saw Chris this morning. He came into the newspaper office and asked about you."

"Me? Why?" Kerri's ears burned.

"Because, he found out I was writing the article about the shop. He wanted to know about you, and he'd heard about the money that was found."

"Did you tell the police this?"

"Yes, of course I did. But that's why I'm worried about you, Kerri. If he did this to Harry for some reason, he might come after you next."

"For what? I don't have anything he could want."

"Maybe there's more money hidden in the shop. Maybe there's evidence of some kind that would link him to his brother's death." He shrugged. "We don't know, because we don't know what might have been hidden there. You didn't know about the money, but it was there."

"You're right. So what's the plan? Tear apart

the walls?"

"No. Find out who does know. The first step I believe, is figuring out if Harry knew something that got him killed. Did he say anything specific to you about what he might be suspicious about?"

"No." She shook her head. "Maybe I should have asked more questions when he mentioned it."

"Don't worry about that now. Let's focus on how we can find out."

"I would think Chris would be the best bet."

"I would agree. But he's also a dangerous man if he is a potential killer."

"Kerri? Kerri, are you okay?" George made his way through the crowd of people to his granddaughter's side.

"Grandpa, I'm glad you're here." She hugged him, though it felt a bit strange to do so.

"I came as soon as I heard. What happened?"

Kerri filled him in on what she knew. "I still can't believe it's true. I just spoke with him this morning. How could he be gone?"

"Try not to think about it too much. It won't make sense for a few days. Actually, it will never make sense, but you'll begin to accept it. I'm sorry I wasn't here earlier." He smiled at Natalie and shot a glance in Steve's direction.

"Oh, Grandpa, this is Steve. He's a local reporter. And this is Natalie, she's a good friend of mine and works at the shop with me. This is George, my grandfather."

The three exchanged handshakes. George's gaze lingered on Steve. "A reporter? Do you know anything about what happened here?"

"No more than what Kerri just told you."

"Ah, I see." He smiled at Natalie. "It's a pleasure to meet you, Natalie."

"You as well."

The police began to rope off the shop. Kerri sighed. "I guess we'd better call it a day, Natalie. We're not getting back in there anytime soon."

"I'll see what I can find out about a timeline

for you, Kerri." Steve walked back towards the shop. George watched him go, then glanced over at Kerri.

"Do you know him well?"

"No, we only met yesterday. But Natalie grew up with him."

"I did. He's a good guy."

"Sure." George nodded.

"Call me if you need anything." Natalie squeezed Kerri's hand then walked off to join the rest of the crowd. George's eyes skimmed the faces in the crowd, then returned to Kerri.

"It looks like you've got yourself quite a dangerous situation here."

Kerri looked into his eyes, then grabbed his hand. She led him away from the crowd to a quiet place behind the next shop. Then she stopped and turned to face him.

"I think it's time you told me the truth."

"The truth about what?"

"About why you're really here."

He lowered his eyes. "I don't know what you mean. I told you, I decided to put down roots."

"Grandpa, that's hard for me to believe. Why now? Why here?"

"Is it so wrong that I want to be near you? I know that we didn't have much of a chance to get to know each other when you were growing up. There were always things pulling me away. I had the same problem with your father. Now, I want a chance to fix that."

"Don't you think it's a little too late?" She bit into her bottom lip.

"Do you?" He searched her eyes. "That's all that really matters. If you don't want me here, then I won't stay."

"It's not that. It's just that I feel like there's more to your presence here."

"Your instincts always were good. I'm here because I want to be close to you, Kerri. But yes, there's a lot I need to tell you. This isn't the time.

Our first priority needs to be figuring out who did this to Harry, and making sure that they're not going to attempt to hurt you."

"I think that you should tell me everything now. I don't like this secrecy. I can't even think straight with everything that's going on. I need you to be honest with me."

"Kerri." He took her hand in his. "I can assure you that I am here to do anything and everything to keep you safe. If you're willing to trust me, then you will just have to accept that this isn't the time to talk about it."

"I guess I have no other choice."

"I can go to the hotel if that will make you more comfortable."

"No, I don't want you to go to the hotel. I just want everything to calm down. I thought I moved here so that I could have some peace. It turns out, I moved into chaos. How can I open my shop if I can't even get inside?" She shook her head. "It was all a mistake."

"It's not a mistake. I think it's a wonderful idea. I'm going to help you get it off the ground. But let's find Harry's murderer first."

"How do you think we're going to do that? It's not as if we're detectives."

"No, we're not. But you and I have always had one thing in common. We're very, very, curious."

"True." She studied him. "But what does that have to do with solving a crime?"

"I say we pay a visit to Harry's family and ask some questions."

"But I barely knew him."

"He died in your shop, it's not out of place for you to offer your condolences to the family."

"Okay, I guess I can do that. But what can I say to them?"

"You'll know when you get there."

"Fine, but I want to see if Natalie will come with us, she knows the family."

"Good idea."

"I also can't go empty-handed. I need to stop at the house first."

"I'll meet you there."

Chapter Six

When Kerri pulled up to her house she noticed the little squirrel from the day before. He perched on the railing of the porch and watched as she approached. She kept waiting for him to run off, but instead he stayed very still. As she climbed up on the porch she reached out a hand towards the squirrel. Their eyes locked, and for a moment she was mesmerized by the way he seemed to look so deep within her. Did he sense all of her conflicting emotions? Or was he just hoping that she would drop more nuts? She was just about to stroke the top of his head when her grandfather's car rumbled into the driveway. The squirrel bolted the instant he heard the car. Kerri frowned. Anyway, it was silly of her to try to pet the squirrel, it was the sort of thing she always did as a child. Kerri unlocked the door and waited for her grandfather to join her. Even though she was frustrated that he wouldn't tell her everything, she was still glad he was there.

"I'm just going to make some toasted pecan cookies to take with us."

"I didn't know you were such a whiz in the kitchen."

"I've learned a lot of different recipes that involve nuts. I like to have them on hand so that when people buy a certain kind of nut I can include a recipe or two that they could use those nuts in."

"What a great idea. You've got such a brilliant mind."

"Not brilliant enough to work out what you're up to."

"Oh, you could, if I wanted you to." He winked at her. She sighed and headed into the kitchen. Cashew chased after her. She reached down and retied the pink bow in Cashew's hair to keep her long hair out of her eyes and then scooped up the dog in her arms. As she licked her cheeks and wriggled in her arms, Kerri finally smiled. It didn't matter what happened in her day, Cashew always managed to make it better. She gave her a treat from the jar on the counter then set her back down on the floor.

After washing up she set about making the pecan cookies. As they baked, the kitchen filled with the lovely, sweet scent of the toasted pecans. She could hear the news that her grandfather watched in the living room. It described Harry's death and where it happened. She cringed when she heard it. Would her shop now be avoided? She set the cookies to cool on the counter then joined her grandfather in the living room.

"Any updates?"

"Nothing new." He shook his head. "I don't know. I get the feeling that the police around here aren't really on their game."

"They're not. There's some strange connection with the police chief. He seems to control everything around here."

"Small towns, sometimes they're not as progressive as the rest of the country. They are often set in their ways. Maybe he thinks he's king."

"Maybe he does." She placed her hands on her hips. "But he's not."

"No, he's not." George nodded and smiled at her. "There's that streak of your mother's."

"What streak?" She perched on the end of the couch and looked at him.

"She is always so riled up by injustice. She'd go after anyone who she thought was corrupt."

"Go after? What do you mean?"

"Oh, ah." He shrugged. "Your mother is a very strong woman."

"What does that mean? She works for charities while Dad is roaming around doing business deals."

"She does a bit more than that, sweetheart." He sighed and took her hand in his. "There are things that your father, mother, and I had to tell you in order to give you the life that we all wanted you to have."

"I have a right to know the truth. I don't know why you would feel the need to hide anything from me."

"It wasn't that we were trying to hide anything from you. It was that we wanted you to have a different kind of life."

She stared at him for some time. Could it be that her grandfather was some kind of criminal? That would be the only reason to lie to her all of those years. If that was the case then maybe the timing of his arrival was more than a coincidence.

"I think we should get these cookies over to Harry's parents' place." She turned and walked back into the kitchen.

She didn't feel comfortable just turning up at Harry's family's house. Even though she hadn't known Natalie long, her instincts told her that she could trust her. She sent her a text about where they were going and asked if she would come with them. A minute later Natalie replied that she would meet them there. When she joined her grandfather at the car, he rubbed her shoulder.

"Don't let it get you down, Kerri. There was nothing you could have done."

"I could have stayed." She bit into her bottom lip. "I could have skipped breakfast, and been there to prevent any of this from happening."

"And whoever killed Harry would have done so at another time. There's no one to blame here, aside from the killer."

She nodded, but her heart was still heavy as she got in the car. He didn't say another word as they drove across town. She tried not to think about what he might reveal to her when he decided he was ready. By the time they walked up to the front door, she'd managed to push down all of her questions. This was about Harry.

"Maybe we should have brought something more than cookies. I mean, is it even appropriate to bring cookies?"

"I think it's just fine. It's very thoughtful."

Kerri nodded, but she wasn't sure. What did her grandfather really know about comforting people? She couldn't remember a single family funeral she'd ever attended, other than her grandmother's. Her grandfather was absent from it as he was too far off the grid in Africa for him to be reached.

"What is that delicious smell?" Natalie walked up to them, and sniffed the air the entire way. "Is that pecans?"

"Toasted pecan cookies, my new specialty." Kerri managed a smile.

"I'm sure that Harry's family will appreciate it, I know I would." She gave Kerri a quick hug. Kerri felt stronger with Natalie there.

Natalie knocked on the door. Kerri stood behind her and held her breath. The door opened a moment later. An older woman with frizzy, gray hair and a warm smile peered out at them.

"Oh, Natalie." She smiled sadly.

"I'm sorry to bother you, Mrs. Jones. We just wanted to say how sorry we are for your loss. This is my friend, Kerri."

"I made you these." Kerri stepped forward and held out the box of cookies in front of her.

"Oh, how sweet." She took the cookies and

stepped back from the door. "Would you like to come inside for a moment."

"Sure, thank you." Natalie stepped in, with Kerri and her grandfather right behind her. Once inside Kerri noticed that there was an older man, and a younger man seated on the couch. She offered a sad smile as they each nodded to her.

Natalie leaned close to her and whispered, "That's Chris."

Kerri's body tensed. Was this the man who might have killed his own brother, and possibly Harry? Would he be bold enough to sit with Harry's parents?

"Look, Mitch, Natalie is here and this kind woman brought us some cookies."

"Cookies?" The older man looked up. "Are they any good?"

"I hope you like them. They're homemade pecan cookies."

"So kind of you to go to so much trouble. Did you know Harry well?" Harry's mother asked.

"Unfortunately no. We'd only met a few times. He was helping me with the shop."

"Oh." She stared at Kerri. "You mean, where he died?"

Kerri nodded.

"You poor dear, that must have been quite a shock for you." Kerri was touched that the woman seemed to worry about her feelings despite the loss she was going through.

"This is Kerri's grandfather, George," Natalie said.

"Here take a seat." Chris stood up to give Kerri and Natalie space on the couch beside Mitch. Kerri smiled briefly at the man who stood up.

"Thanks, Chris." Natalie nodded to Chris.

"Thank you," Kerri murmured as she sat down beside Natalie. Her grandfather stayed near the door.

"I'm Chris." He offered his hand to her. "A friend of the family's."

"Chris." Kerri took his hand in a quick shake.

"You run the shop my brother used to own," Chris said.

"I'm sorry for your loss as well." Kerri looked at him.

"I guess this has been rather difficult for you with two murders."

"Yes, it has. I can't help but wonder, if Len and Harry..." Kerri started.

"Don't. Let me stop you right there. It's easy to make that assumption, but no. Len's death and Harry's death are not related. Len was killed in a botched robbery. Harry was killed in cold blood."

"Oh." Harry's mother placed a hand over her mouth as she returned from the kitchen.

"I'm so sorry. It isn't appropriate of me to talk about that." Chris cringed and wiped a hand across his face. "It's just that all of this is so much. First Len, now Harry. It doesn't fit. Why would anyone want to hurt Harry?"

"Have you really thought about that?" George stepped up beside Kerri. "Who might have wanted to hurt him?"

"Of course I have. Harry was a friendly guy. He was always willing to help people out if he could. I can't tell you how many things he fixed over the years free of charge, at our homes, or at the shop. He didn't do anything to deserve this," Chris said.

"I'm sure he didn't." Kerri lowered her eyes. "I hope that the police are able to figure this out, and fast."

"The police," Mitch sputtered. "What are they going to do for our son? They never do a thing. Nothing." His hands balled into fists.

"That isn't the case. The police are already investigating." Kerri looked into his eyes. "They have the shop roped off and are collecting evidence. I'm sure they will figure it out."

"No. They don't want to figure it out. That's the problem. They just want the case to go away. Just like with Len. How could a man just be killed, and his murderer never be caught? Now Harry is gone, and it will be the same thing. They will toss him aside just like they tossed Len aside."

"Don't say that, Mitch." His wife sat down on the chair beside him. "We have to believe that Harry's killer will be found. If we don't then we might as well give up on him."

"Yes, Norma, if you say so." He patted her hand. "Whatever you say."

Kerri met her grandfather's eyes. "We should go."

Natalie nodded and stood up as well. She offered her condolences to Mitch and Norma once more.

"Thank you for stopping by." Mitch stood up and held out his hand to George. George gave it a solid shake and looked into his eyes.

"I'm sure there will be justice for your son. I know it won't do much to ease your loss."

"No, it won't." Mitch sighed. As they left the house Kerri looked at her grandfather.

"That was very touching."

"I meant it." He paused beside the car.

"There's nothing that bothers me more than someone getting away with hurting someone else, especially murder."

"I didn't know that about you."

George smiled at her as he waited for her to get into the car. "There's a lot of things that you don't know just yet, Kerri." Kerri studied him for a moment, then turned to Natalie.

"Thanks for coming with us."

"Anytime, Kerri. I'm sorry this happened."

"Me too." She shook her head. "I just wish there was some clue as to who did this."

"We'll figure it out, Kerri." Natalie gave her a hug. "Call me if you want to talk."

"Thanks, Nat." She waved to her friend as she got in the car with her grandfather.

On the drive back to her house Kerri bit the tip of her tongue to hold back a barrage of questions. Her grandfather already made it clear that he was not going to tell her anything before he was ready. But the suspense was difficult to tolerate. She tried to take her mind off it by focusing on the investigation.

"What did you think of Chris? Steve suspects that he might have had something to do with Len's death."

"It's hard to say. He strikes me as genuine, but killers are often charismatic. I think Harry is going to hold the key."

"But Harry's gone."

"He is. But his house isn't. His belongings can tell us what he can't."

"Yes, but his belongings are in his house."

"I agree."

Kerri looked over at him with wide eyes. "Are you suggesting that we break in?"

He glanced over at her, then looked back through the windshield. "Sounds to me like you just suggested it."

"Grandpa, we can't break in."

"Okay." He shrugged. "It was your idea."

Kerri's mouth dropped open. She wanted to argue the point, but saw no benefit to it. "It would be crazy. The police are investigating his murder. If we were to break in, we could become the prime suspects."

"You have an alibi."

"You don't."

He pulled into the driveway of her house and nodded. "You're right. I don't."

"What were you doing all morning, Grandpa?" She made no move to get out of the car. He turned the engine off and met her eyes.

"Am I a suspect now?" He grinned. She didn't smile in return.

"You're secretive, you showed up out of the blue, and you seem very interested in Harry." She set her jaw as she looked into his eyes. "I think it makes sense to ask a few questions."

"I'm not a killer, Kerri. You must know that?"

"But you are here for a reason."

"I'm here for you." He raised an eyebrow. "It's

up to you whether you believe that or not."

Kerri dropped her gaze to her hands and sighed. "I'm sorry, I shouldn't have questioned you."

"Don't be sorry, Kerri." He waited until she looked up at him then smiled. "If there is anything on this earth I can ever truly teach you, it's to question everything, and everyone. Never take things at face value. There's almost always something hidden underneath."

She peered at him as her ears burned. For the first time she realized that her grandfather was a bundle of secrets. Maybe she'd always known that, as he'd always fascinated her. How to get to the answers was something she hadn't worked out just yet.

Chapter Seven

Kerri put together dinner for her and her grandfather while trying to sort through her thoughts. Just as she set the plates on the table her cell phone rang. When she saw that it was Steve, she excused herself and stepped outside. Cashew followed after her.

"Hi, Steve."

"Kerri, I hope you don't mind the call. I just wanted to fill you in on what I found out."

"Not at all. What did you find?"

"Chris and Len had a falling out over money. Something to do with the business deal, so their partnership plans fell through. I can't determine exactly what happened, but I was able to gather that Chris wasn't happy about something, and Len wasn't happy that Chris wasn't happy."

"Okay. So, maybe Len was involved in something that Chris didn't think was right," Kerri said.

"Maybe. But would it lead him to kill his brother?"

"Let's say it didn't. Maybe he suspected that Harry killed his brother."

"I hadn't thought of that," Steve said.

"If Chris and Len were as close as people say, then maybe Chris wanted to get his revenge."

"But Harry was never even a suspect in Len's murder."

"Was anyone?" Kerri asked.

"His wife."

"Len's wife?"

"Yes. Briefly. I think the spouse always is. She wasn't home when Len was killed. She came home to find the house broken into and Len dead, but she didn't have an alibi. She was checking on her parents' house because they were away on vacation. When she came home she found Len's body, and called the police," Steve said.

"So, no one can vouch for the fact that she wasn't at the home at the time of the murder?"

"No, but she was cleared by the chief."

"Ah yes, the chief who decides everything in this town?"

"It's not as bad as that. He's just rather protective."

"Well, from what I can tell the police seem to be covering up both of these murders. First they did almost nothing to solve Len's murder, now, they seem to be dropping the ball on Harry's. Is anyone even investigating it? If Chris is a suspect, why was he sitting in Harry's parents' house with them?"

"Did you go to see them?"

"Yes, I did."

"You should have taken me with you."

"My grandfather went with me and so did Natalie."

"They did? Did you find out anything?"

"Only that Chris seemed very close to them. I don't know if I can believe that Chris would kill Harry and then go sit with his parents."

"He would if he was trying to come across as innocent or maybe he was there for another reason."

"Maybe. I'll let you know if I find out anything else."

"Okay, please do. I want to have my thumb on this."

"I think that we have to remember that it's not just a story, it's someone's life."

"I know that. I can assure you, I'm not involved in this with any ill-intent."

"That's good." As she hung up the phone she hoped that was the case. Steve struck her as the type that was motivated to get whatever he wanted. He might want to solve the case, but he also wanted to be the first to break the story. She hoped he would consider Harry's family's feelings before anything else. When she stepped back into the house her grandfather was still at the dinner table. She sat down with him again and he met her eyes.

"Who was that?"

"Steve."

"The reporter?"

"Yes. He called to let me know that there was a financial rift between Chris and Len. Something to do with the business. In fact, they were at odds when Len was killed."

"Well, that's a pretty good motive for murder then."

"Yet, Chris isn't a suspect. The only person they investigated briefly was Len's wife, because she found the body."

"Interesting. Maybe the wife and the brother were working together."

"Do you really think that's possible?"

"I've seen worse, trust me," George said.

Kerri wiped her mouth with a napkin and sat back in her chair. "Okay, out with it. I'm not taking no for an answer. I don't care if you don't think it's the right time. I need to know what is going on."

"I can see that. Your ears are as red as tomatoes." He laughed. "I used to tell you that you could lead Santa's sleigh with them, remember?"

"Yes." She reached up and rubbed her ear. "I wore earmuffs for a week after you said that."

"Why?"

"I thought Santa might whisk me away."

"Oops." He chuckled. "All right." He took a deep breath and looked across the table at her. "I will tell you the truth. I understand that this is going to sound very strange to you. It also might upset you. However, it's been necessary to keep this a secret. I am retired now and I want you to know the truth, although I will expect you to keep it to yourself."

"What is it, Grandpa? Whatever it is, I'm sure that I can handle it."

"I was never actually a curator of a museum. That was my cover story."

"Cover story?"

"I was a spy."

"A spy?" Kerri's breath caught in her throat. "You're kidding right?" Natalie's voice echoed through her mind. Maybe her grandfather was getting a little senile.

"I'm afraid not. Now that you're an adult, I can tell you the truth."

"Wait a minute. This can't possibly be true. I would have known."

"No. You wouldn't have. That's why you were at boarding school. It's why your parents were constantly moving."

"My parents? How are they involved?"

"Your father is..." George paused and frowned. "We're at odds about this, but you're an adult, and I feel it's best to tell you the whole truth. He is an active agent. That's why you don't see or hear from him much. I know that it was likely a very difficult childhood for you. If it gives you any comfort, your father had the same childhood, as did I. It's a bit of a tradition in our family."

"I don't understand how you could have kept this from me all of these years. Why would you lie to me? Why would you keep me in the dark?"

"Because we wanted this for you." He gestured to the house. "Your mother was worried that if you knew what the family business was, you'd want to follow in those footsteps. She wanted a normal life for you, without all the stress and secrecy that comes from the life she married into."

"What about Mom? Does she have something to do with this kind of work, too?"

"Not exactly. She is involved, but doesn't work as a spy. A lot of her charity work actually serves as a way to gather information that she gave to your father and me when we needed it. Sometimes she asked us to use our skills in certain areas in different parts of the world to help a cause that didn't necessarily interest our bosses."

"Then in a way she is a spy, too." Kerri frowned. "I guess I don't know her at all."

"Don't say that." He reached across the table

and took her hand. "Don't ever say that. You know your mother better than anyone else. I can tell, because you emulate her so clearly in your personality and actions. You believe in peace, and justice, and fairness. Someone lesser than you would have tried to keep all of that money for yourself."

She pursed her lips. "I never said how much money it was."

"I just assumed it was a lot."

"So, now we're back to secrets?"

"Okay fine. I did access the police database and I know how much money was there. But I did that so I could get an idea of what kind of danger you're in. The higher the dollar amount, the more likely someone is to kill for it."

"Maybe that's true, but there was no more money at the shop. So, why did Harry need to die?"

"I don't know." George shook his head. "There must have been some other motive. You said

Harry offered to do the job free of charge?"

"Yes, he did."

"That's a big job to do for free. I bet there was something in that shop that he wanted. Maybe we should take a look around."

"But the police have it taped off."

"You're the owner aren't you?" He lifted an eyebrow.

"Yes, but I don't want to interfere in the investigation."

"We'll be careful. Why don't we go take a peek now?"

"Grandpa, I don't know. What if we get caught?"

"I have a little bit of experience in being sneaky. Remember?"

She stared across the table at him. The very thought of him being a spy was hard for her to fathom. Could he be telling the truth, or was this some kind of elaborate ruse? In a way it made sense to her. It explained the absences as she grew up. But it was still hard to swallow.

"I suppose you do. It is my store, after all. I guess we should have a look around."

"Sounds like the perfect after-dinner adventure."

Chapter Eight

It was hard for Kerri not to think about everything that her grandfather revealed. As much as she wanted to work out what had happened to Harry, her own life had just been turned upside down. She drove towards the store, with her grandfather silent beside her. There was so much to figure out and yet she wasn't sure that she was going to get to the bottom of any of it. When she pulled into the parking lot, her grandfather directed her to the back of the building. She parked in a space from which she could still see the road.

"Let's go." She started to open the door.

"No, I don't think that's a good idea." He put his hand over hers. "Just give it a few minutes."

"Okay." She sat back and looked through the window at the dark shop. The bright yellow police tape was enough to remind her that even though she owned the shop, it didn't belong to her at that moment.

"Are you okay, Kerri?"

"I will be, once all of this is sorted out."

"Don't worry, we'll get there."

"How long are we going to sit in the car?"

"Be patient."

"But there's no one here. What are we waiting for?"

He tapped the windshield. "Just watch."

Kerri sighed and slunk back against the seat. As anxious as she was, it was hard to sit still. With the shop right in front of her, she wanted to get in and get it over with.

"Grandpa?"

"There it is." He pointed towards the road as a patrol car drove slowly past.

"How did you know?" She shifted down in the seat to hide her face.

"Any closed off crime scene will be part of a patrol officer's loop. So, if I'm correct we should have at least forty-five minutes before he comes back around."

"And if you're not?"

"You do know how to run, right?"

"Ugh."

"Don't worry, kid. We can do this. Even if we're caught, you can just tell them that you left something in the shop you had to get. It's no big deal."

"Maybe not to you, but I've never been in any kind of trouble. I can't even imagine being in handcuffs."

"You won't be." He locked eyes with her. "I can promise you that."

She sighed and opened the car door. "Now we have forty minutes, let's hurry." They made their way to the back door. Kerri slid her key into the lock, then ducked under the police tape. Her grandfather followed after her. Once inside it struck her that the last time she was there she had found Harry dead. Her stomach churned with the thought. She didn't realize that she staggered until her grandfather caught her by the arm.

"Are you okay?"

"Yes. Sorry. I just keep thinking about Harry."

"That's good. That's why we're here. Just focus on the evidence, not the crime. Okay? We need to find what Harry might have been looking for, and what his killer might have hoped to find."

"Okay." She nodded. "He volunteered to help me finish the floors. But I was only gone for about an hour. I'm sure that he didn't get very far."

"Let's take a look."

Kerri led her grandfather through the back room into the main store area. "He didn't do anything at all." She stared at the piles of wood on the floor.

"Yes, he did. He did something. We just have to determine what." He picked his way across the open floorboards.

"Look Grandpa." She pointed to a piece of the molding along the floor that had been pulled away. "I didn't ask him to do that. He was just supposed to do the floorboards."

"That's it. It was important enough that he pulled it away first. Here." He pulled a flashlight off his keychain and handed it to her. "Take a look."

Kerri crouched down and flicked the light into the open space behind the molding. "Whatever was here is gone now."

"Are you sure? There isn't anything left behind?"

She reached her hand inside the space and felt around. When her fingertips touched paper she grabbed it and pulled it out. "I found something."

"What is it?"

She trained the flashlight beam on it. "It looks like the same money bands that were around the bundles of money I found."

"So, there was more. That's why Harry offered to help. He knew it would be there. That's why the killer attacked him here. Maybe he waited for

Harry to find the money, then swooped in and took care of two problems."

"So, you're still thinking Chris?"

"Is there anyone else to consider?" George asked.

"It's hard to say just yet. But we should turn these into the police."

"If we do, they'll know that we were here when we shouldn't have been."

"Are you saying we should hide the evidence?"

"I'm not saying that. But ask yourself this, why didn't the police find it? It took us a few minutes. Why didn't they look inside that open hole?" George asked.

"You think that there's a cover-up going on here?"

"Either that or very spotty police work. Maybe this chief that seems to be in control of everything in this town had a reason to not find Len's killer, and now Harry's. I think it's something we need to consider."

"That's a terrible thought."

"Corruption affects many people in power, Kerri. I've seen it more than once."

"What did I move into?"

"A lovely town, that needs a sharp mind, and a good dose of justice."

Kerri sighed and tucked the bands into her purse. "I guess we're on our own with this."

"Together we can figure it out. Let's go. It's better not to linger."

"Wait, I just want to grab some things from the office. I received some deliveries and I didn't log them. If I don't, I'll forget."

"Okay, I'll wait here for you."

Kerri stepped into the darkened office and began to quickly sort through the paperwork on her desk. She tried not to think about what had happened to Harry. Once she had the paperwork she needed she headed to the back door where her grandfather waited.

"I have everything I need." She took a glance around the shop that she had hoped to open soon. If Harry's murder went unsolved, would she ever feel comfortable opening it? Did she even want to in a town where the police might be so corrupt? George opened the back door to step outside. The next thing Kerri saw was a flurry of movement and the sound of skin striking skin. She pointed the flashlight at the two men rolling on the ground.

"Grandpa! Stop!"

George stumbled to his feet, but kept his fists up. "He came at me, Kerri."

"Because I didn't know who was coming out of a closed off crime scene." Steve wiped some blood from his bottom lip. "What are you two doing here?"

Kerri frowned as she looked between the two men. "What are we doing here? What are you doing here, Steve?"

He cleared his throat. "I was just going to take a look around."

"Were you?" She met his eyes. "At a closed crime scene?"

"I'm a reporter. I want the facts."

"Or you were hoping there was still some money left behind. You knew there was more, didn't you, Steve? Or maybe you came back to cover your tracks?" George said.

"Grandpa, I don't think…"

"Just like you happened to show up when there was a ton of money to find. You don't think that's a little coincidental?" Steve asked.

"Look, we can't stand here and argue about this. The patrol car will be making its rounds again soon. We can figure this out somewhere else," George said.

"No thanks. I'll be on my way." Steve stepped past George and continued across the parking lot.

"Steve, wait!"

"Don't." George put his hand on Kerri's shoulder. "His pride is wounded, he's not coming back."

"Why did you hit him?" Kerri swatted at his arm.

"I didn't know who he was. He came at me as I was coming out. All I knew was he wasn't a cop. He could have been the killer." He frowned. "He still could be. Why else do you think he was here?"

"He was here to get a story. That's the only reason, Grandpa. I don't think he's involved in all of this."

"You don't think he is, but you don't know that he isn't. If you really want to get to the bottom of this then you have to keep an open mind about who might be involved. The truth is, you don't really know anyone here."

Kerri sighed. "I hate to admit it, but you're right. I don't want to think poorly of anyone, but I don't really know who they are. Just like, I don't really know who you are."

"You do. You know the important parts. Maybe you didn't know what I did for a profession, but you knew me as a person. I hope you can see it that way."

"All I know for sure is I've been lied to for a long time. How can I expect to spot a liar now if I've never been able to spot one my entire life?"

"You have great instincts, Kerri. I wasn't lying about that. You've always been able to tell when someone has a good heart. Maybe that's why you didn't find out the truth about your family, because you knew, deep down, that whatever we were hiding, it wasn't to hurt you."

"I think I just need to sleep a little. I'm pretty exhausted. We can go over everything again in the morning."

"You're right, let's get you home."

The drive home was awkward and tense. Kerri had so much she wanted to say, yet no energy to say it. She barely mumbled goodnight to her grandfather before she headed off to bed herself. She closed the door to her bedroom and closed her eyes. Her grandfather slept in the next room. He was a man she had admired her entire life. She wasn't going to let the secrets he kept change the way she felt about him. For the first time in a very long time she felt close to someone in her family. He was there when she needed him the most, and that meant a lot to her. Cashew jumped up onto the bed beside her and nuzzled her hand until she began to pet her.

"What a crazy night, Cash. I'm not sure what to think."

Cashew wagged her tail.

"I know, I know. We need to have some fun, don't we? I'll take you for a walk first thing in the morning."

Kerri stretched out in bed and curled her arm around her dog. Cashew's soft snores ushered her into a deep sleep.

Chapter Nine

When Kerri woke the next morning her head ached with the weight of what had happened the night before. Now she was almost certain that Harry was murdered for money that was hidden in her shop. What if there was more? What if the murderer was someone she already knew in the town? The very thought of interacting with a killer made her stomach ache right along with her head. For a few minutes she lost herself in the possibility that she'd made a huge mistake. Buying the house and the shop depleted quite a bit of her funds. It wasn't as if she could just change her mind, pack up, and leave. Her life was here now, and she had to find a way to make that work.

Kerri pushed herself to shower, dress, and grab a muffin for breakfast. Then she hooked Cashew onto her leash and headed out for a morning walk. She was relieved that her grandfather was not yet awake. When she stepped outside Cashew began to tug at the leash. She stuck her nose to the ground and sniffed, then tugged again. Kerri let the dog take the lead and ended up in the driveway beside the house. Right away she spotted the little squirrel that stole her nuts. He perched on the top of a fence post and stared at her with dark, wide eyes.

"You again. I'm starting to think that you might like me. Or is it my nuts?" She grinned and pulled a piece of her muffin off. She held it out to the squirrel. The squirrel leaned close. She set it down on the fence where he could reach it. The squirrel snapped it right up. Its little cheeks worked faster than she'd ever seen before. "Oh, you like that, huh?" She broke off another piece for him. "I bet you see everything around here, don't you? If only you could talk, I'm sure you'd have a lot to tell me about everyone in this town."

The squirrel fluffed his bushy tail. It seemed to her that he was offering her some comfort. "Maybe you would know if Chris and Len fought. Maybe you would know who walked into the shop after I left." Her eyes widened as she uttered those words aloud. "That's it! All we need to do is find out who entered the shop after I left. Maybe there are some cameras nearby that can give us a clue. Also, I can call and check with the driver who made the deliveries. He might have seen or heard something, too. Thanks for the idea!"

She took Cashew on her walk, then returned to the house just in time to find her grandfather with two fresh cups of coffee.

"Good morning, Kerri. I thought you might like some coffee."

"I would, thank you." She took the coffee from him and leaned against the counter. "I think we should see if we can get any surveillance video from near the shop that might show who was in the area near the shop, or maybe even who went inside."

"That's a good idea. I'm guessing Len didn't have a camera installed and you don't have any kind of camera up yet."

"To be honest I hadn't even given much

thought to putting one in. I didn't think security would be that much of an issue here."

"Don't let a quiet neighborhood lull you into taking risks. Crime happens everywhere, even in the nicest places."

"I suppose you're right."

"Kerri, I know you're still adjusting to everything I told you, but I hope you know nothing has changed. I'm still your grandfather, I'm still here for you, no other reason."

"I believe you, Grandpa. There are many questions I want answered, but they can wait. Honestly, I'm just glad that you're here to help figure this out with me."

"Let's head into town and see what we can find out. It wouldn't hurt to find out what we can about Len, Chris, and Harry as well."

"You know the best resource for that would be Steve, although after last night I'm not sure that he's going to be talkative."

"I'm sorry, I did what I thought I had to do.

Besides, Kerri, he can't be ruled out as a suspect."

"Neither can you." She met his eyes. "But that doesn't mean I suspect you."

"I should hope not." He smiled.

"I'm going to make a few quick calls, then we can go into town." She retreated to her room with her cell phone and found the paperwork that she brought home from the office. From the invoice she was able to get the phone number for the delivery service. She dialed the number and waited for someone to answer.

"Packages Fast." The gruff voice was not exactly welcoming.

"I was wondering if you could give me the name of the driver who delivered my packages yesterday."

"If you have a complaint you can log it with me."

"No, I don't have a complaint, just a question. Could you please give me his information?"

"You're talking to him. I'm the owner and

operator."

"You're the only driver?"

"Currently. I fired two guys last week."

"So, you made the delivery to my shop?" She gave her name and the address of the store.

"Yes, I did."

"Are you aware that a murder occurred there?"

"I heard about it."

"When you came to the shop did you see or hear anything unusual? Did you see anyone go in or out?"

"No. I didn't see or hear anything."

"Are you sure?"

"Look, lady, I answered your questions." He hung up the phone. She was a little startled by how harsh he was. On a hunch she looked up the name of the company and found his name. Frank Gerard. She made a note of the name and returned to her grandfather in the kitchen. She would follow up on it later.

"Let's see if we can find ourselves some footage from near the shop."

"Good plan." He nodded.

Chapter Ten

Kerri drove into town with her grandfather in the passenger seat. That felt surreal enough on its own, but when she rolled past the shop and saw a pile of flowers and teddy bears by the front of the door, she wondered if she might still be dreaming.

"It looks like someone set up a memorial for Harry. He must have been well-liked," George said.

"I haven't met anyone yet who wasn't fond of him." Kerri was about to drive to the local police station to find out if they'd checked surveillance footage from the time of the murder and if there was any other information Detective Meyers was prepared to reveal, when she noticed Natalie's car in the parking lot of the florist. "Do you mind if we stop for a moment? I want to see how she's doing."

"No, I don't mind at all."

She parked beside Natalie's car and led the way into the shop. Natalie stood close to the counter. "It's very sweet what everyone is doing, but I wondered if you noticed anyone unusual purchasing flowers."

"Unusual?" The shop owner leaned on the counter. "What would make someone unusual?"

"Maybe someone you didn't recognize, or someone you wouldn't expect to buy flowers."

"No, not really." He paused, then looked at Kerri and smiled. "Something I can help you with?"

"Kerri!" Natalie turned to face her with a smile. "I was just going to call you."

"I see that you noticed the memorial." Kerri smiled in return.

"Yes, I thought I'd do a little investigating. But it hasn't led me anywhere."

"It's a good start."

"Are you sure there wasn't anyone suspicious, maybe someone you don't know from around town?" Natalie asked.

"I'm sorry, no." He smiled at the door as the

bell above it rang to signal that someone else had arrived. Kerri turned to see a woman step inside. She looked to be in her thirties. From the pearls around her neck to the silky pants suit she wore, her entire presence spoke of class.

"Morning, Bob. I do hope you have some fresh flowers left."

"I always have flowers for you, Delores. How are you today?"

"Unsettled, as I'm sure everyone else is. Hello, Natalie." She nodded to Natalie.

"Good morning, Delores. This is Kerri and George." Natalie looked between them. Delores looked from Kerri to George and then offered a brief smile. "Are you buying flowers for the memorial?" Natalie asked.

"No, actually. I think there are enough flowers out there already. I'm buying some flowers to take to Len's grave. I have every week since his death."

"That's a beautiful way to honor him," Natalie said.

"Thank you." She reached into her pocket and pulled out some money. As she did, Kerri noticed something flutter to the floor. She reached down to pick it up and return it to Delores, but when she saw what it was, she tucked it into her own pocket instead.

"Have a good day, Delores." Bob nodded to her as she walked out. Once she was gone he looked over at Natalie. "Such a sad story. She loved her husband so much. I'm sure that she would have done anything to protect him."

"I'm sure." Natalie nodded.

"That was Len's wife?" Kerri peered out the window and watched as the woman disappeared into her car. "How sad. Did you know Len well?" She turned back to Bob.

"Quite well. He was a good guy. Of course, not everyone would agree with that."

"Was there anyone in particular that might have had a problem with him?"

"You mean other than Detective Meyers?" He

chuckled.

"Detective Meyers?" Kerri rested her hands on the counter. "He had a problem with Len?"

"A huge problem. He made it his mission to get Len put away."

"Put away for what?"

"I'm not sure that I should be talking about this." He shrugged. "I guess it doesn't matter now, since he's already gone. When I first heard he was dead I wondered if Detective Meyers finally caught up with him."

"Wait, why did you think Detective Meyers would be involved in Len's death?" George looked him straight in the eye.

"Because he'd been trying to take down Len for some time. He was convinced that Len was running an illegal fencing ring through his pawn shop, but he couldn't prove it. He'd interviewed me a few times about people I saw coming and going. I thought maybe he got fed up enough to shoot him."

Kerri's ears burned as she stared at Bob. "But now you don't think that's the case?"

"Well, of course not. Detective Meyers might have had a bone to pick with Len, but he's not the type to shoot a man in cold blood. Maybe if Len had attacked him, or something, but he wouldn't break into a man's house and kill him."

"Interesting. What about the people that you saw coming and going, was there ever anything that came of that?" Kerri asked.

"It wasn't really the people, it was the timing. It was always after dark when the shop was closed. I'd see a car here and there pull into the pawn shop. I never thought much of it, but when Detective Meyers started asking me about it, I decided to pay closer attention."

"So, you think this Detective Meyers is an honest fellow?" George narrowed his eyes. "I've heard the chief isn't."

"The chief has been the chief for many years and he is on a bit of a power trip, but he'll be retiring next year. Rumor is Detective Meyers might move up and take his place."

"Very interesting." Kerri reached up and rubbed one of her ears. "Thanks for the information."

The three left the shop. As soon as they were outside Kerri looked towards her shop, which was still roped off by yellow tape. "Does anyone else think that a promotion could be good motivation to take someone's life?"

"It could be." George nodded.

"I don't know. Detective Meyers is a lot of things, but I don't think he could be a killer." Natalie shook her head. "Just because he was after Len doesn't mean he would kill him, and I really don't think he would have done anything to hurt Harry."

"It's easy for someone in a position of power to fool others. He could easily cover up his own involvement. Maybe that's why both of the cases seem to have not been thoroughly investigated." George crossed his arms.

"I think it's something we need to consider," Kerri said.

"I do, too. Let's continue on to the police station and see what we can find out."

"Wait a minute." Natalie laughed. "You think you're going to walk right in there and question a detective?"

"And the chief, if he's in." Kerri nodded. "It's the only thing we can do at this point. There is no harm in asking a few questions."

"Then you should call Steve."

"That might not be the best idea." Kerri grimaced.

"Why not? Did something happen?"

George lowered his eyes and scuffed his shoe against the sidewalk. "You could say that."

"My grandfather split his lip." Kerri sighed.

"Huh?" Natalie grinned. "You're not serious!"

"I'm afraid so."

"Wow. I can see how that might cause a bit of

a problem. But I would give him a call anyway. If he thinks he can get information for a story he'll make a deal with The Devil, or just someone who split his lip. Besides, he's a good guy, he doesn't hold grudges."

"I guess I could try. Thanks, Natalie. I'll update you as soon as we know anything."

"Great." She waved as she walked off. Kerri selected Steve's name on her phone and started to hit call.

"Do you think that's a good idea? I'm not sure if I trust him. He could be in on all of this."

"He could be, or he could be our only way into more information. I didn't want to say anything while Natalie was here, but look what fell out of Delores' pocket." She pulled the paper money bands out of her purse to show him. "Don't they look like the ones we found last night?"

"Yes, they do." He peered closely at one of them. "I'd say identical."

"So, how did she end up with these in her

pocket?"

"Maybe she has the missing money." George snapped his fingers. "I bet she took Harry out and grabbed the money for herself."

"I think that's possible."

"Maybe she suspected that Harry killed Len, and decided to take revenge. It could have been a lucky coincidence that she found the money at the same time."

"Maybe." Kerri walked back towards the car. "I think we should find out what we can about the original investigation. I know the best way we can do that."

"Steve?"

"Steve."

He sighed. "All right, if you think it's best. Let's give him a call."

Kerri hit the call button before she started the car.

She waited through three rings with the full expectation that Steve would ignore her call.

When she heard his voice she was surprised that it wasn't automated.

"Kerri, is your grandfather looking for round two?"

"No, I'm sorry about that, Steve. It was an accident."

"I know. But it still doesn't explain what you were doing snooping around. You could have easily been caught."

"I'm not worried about that right now. All I care about is finding the truth and getting my shop open."

"I can understand that. I feel the same way, I want to find out the truth. So, what's the plan?"

"You'll help me?"

"Of course I will." She gave her grandfather a thumbs up, then continued.

"Can you meet us at the police station? We want to see if we can speak with the police chief or Detective Meyers."

"Ah, getting daring. Absolutely." Kerri was

relieved to hear that he seemed eager to help her and decided to ask him for help with something else.

"Can you also find out some information about someone for me please? His name is Frank Gerard."

"Frankie? Why do you want to know anything about him?"

"You know him?"

"I know of him. He lives out of town, but he has a reputation around town. It's not a good one."

"He delivered packages to the store around the time Harry was killed."

"Interesting. I didn't know he started a business. I'll look into it and let you know what I find out."

"Thanks, Steve. I think he might know something that he is not saying."

"No problem. I'll see if I can find any information on Frankie and then I'll meet you at the station in about thirty minutes."

"Great, see you there, Steve." She smiled as she hung up the phone. Her grandfather tipped his head to the side.

"Have you really only known him for a short time?"

"Why?" She looked over at him.

"The way you smile after you talk to him..."

"Stop, Grandpa. I'm just glad that he wants to help us, after what you did."

"You mean saving you from an unknown assailant? Yes, you're welcome."

She grinned as she turned to look out the window.

"Steve will be at the station in about thirty minutes so why don't we walk around the area near the shop to see if we can spot any surveillance cameras."

"Good idea!"

After walking within the vicinity of the shop

they could not find one camera.

"This is unbelievable," Kerri said with frustration. "Haven't they heard of surveillance?"

"Doesn't look like it."

"Let's head over to the station, Steve should be there soon."

"Good idea," George said as they got in the car.

Chapter Eleven

Within a few minutes Kerri and her grandfather were parked outside the police station.

"We should probably wait until Steve gets here." As she spoke Steve walked towards them along the sidewalk. He pulled his sunglasses off and tucked them into his shirt, then squinted into the car.

"Are you sure you're up for this?" He raised an eyebrow. "You're going to have to have thick skin."

"I'm sure I can handle it." Kerri stepped out of the car. Her grandfather followed after. Steve took a step back and put his hands in the air.

"Don't worry, I'm keeping my distance."

"Relax, Steve, I'm no loose cannon." George offered him his hand. "I'm sorry about the mix-up."

Steve stared at him for a moment, then

nodded. "All right. I am sorry, too." The two shook hands. Kerri breathed a sigh of relief.

"All right, let me do the talking. I can get us a meeting with Detective Meyers. I'm not sure how long of a meeting, or what he'll share, but I can get us in," Steve said.

"You do that." George nodded. His gaze swept the entire lobby. Kerri noticed the way he seemed to take in everything at once. She wished she was as observant. Steve disappeared down a hallway. A few minutes later he returned and gestured for them to follow him. Kerri fell into step behind him, but George hesitated.

"Grandpa, aren't you coming?"

"You go ahead. He'll be more comfortable talking to you. I'll wait here."

She sensed that he was up to something, but Steve neared a corner and she didn't want to lose track of him. "Okay. Don't get yourself into trouble."

"Me?" He smiled.

She frowned, but followed after Steve. When she caught up to him, he turned to look at her.

"Wait, I wanted to tell you what I found out about Frankie. It might be nothing, but it might be something. He has a long record, and a few of his arrests coincided with a few of Len's. I think they might have worked together at one point."

"Is there any connection to Harry?"

"Not that I could find. In fact, most of the recent information that I found pointed to Frankie turning his life around, so I don't see what motivation he would have to hurt Harry, but I can tell you if hc saw something, he's probably not going to say a word about it."

"Because he doesn't trust the police."

"Exactly." He opened a door to one of the interrogation rooms. The bare walls and dim lighting left Kerri feeling uneasy. "Are you going to stay?"

He smiled. "I hoped that you might want me to."

"Great." Kerri nodded and sat down at the table. Steve paced back and forth as they waited.

"Just remember, he's doing us a favor by even speaking to us."

"I know." She fiddled with her cell phone and opened a recording program so that she wouldn't miss a word of what the detective said. Once she had it on, she glanced over at Steve. The more she looked at him the more attractive he became. Despite the fact that she didn't know him very well she felt like she could trust him. Maybe it was because they both wanted to find out who the murderer was. The door opened and Detective Meyers stepped inside. He looked from Steve, to Kerri, then back to Steve again.

"This is all off the record, understand?"

"Yes, I understand."

Kerri slid her phone into her purse so that he wouldn't notice the recording application. He sat down across from them.

"What can I help you with?"

"It's about Harry's death, and possibly Len's, too." Kerri locked eyes with him.

"Oh? Do you know something about them?"

"I just wanted to know what is happening with the investigations and maybe why Len's death wasn't investigated more."

"Look, the chief decides where to allocate the resources. He didn't think that it was worth pursuing the investigation further because we weren't making much progress."

"But you felt differently didn't you?"

"I would like every murder to be solved. But the truth is, that's more of a dream than a reality. I have to work with what I have, even if that means that I have to let some things go for the moment."

"So, there's no validity to the idea that you were trying to catch Len in a criminal act?"

He cleared his throat and eyed her for a long moment. "What are you talking about?"

"I think you know what I'm talking about. You

knew that Len was involved in something criminal. He was a fence. You wanted to catch him."

"I couldn't ever prove anything significant enough to stick. He was arrested, but he always managed to get the charges dropped."

"That must have been frustrating," Steve spoke up.

"Yes, of course it was. He was bringing a criminal element into this town that could have proved very dangerous to everyone that lives here."

"With Len gone, you wouldn't have to worry about him drawing criminals in." Steve tilted his head to the side.

"Steve, you know me better than that." He stared into his eyes. "What are you implying?"

"We just want to get this solved," Steve said and held his hands up in surrender.

"Did you look at the surveillance footage of who entered and exited my shop around the time of Harry's murder?" Kerri asked, trying to break the tension.

"We would have, if there was any." Detective Meyers looked at her.

"There's no footage at all?" Kerri asked.

"No." Detective Meyers shook his head. Kerri wasn't surprised considering the fact that neither she nor her grandfather had found any cameras. "People don't expect trouble around here and we prefer not to feel like we are always being watched. So, there are very few surveillance cameras around town."

"That's very convenient, isn't it?" Steve asked.

"We're done here." Detective Meyers stood up from the table. "I know what you're implying and I'm not going to tolerate these accusations. I thought you came here for a little bit more information about the store you bought, Kerri, and the crimes that have been committed there. Had I known Steve had some crazy idea in his head that I had something to do with Len's death, I wouldn't have bothered to agree to the meeting."

He looked at Steve. "You know better, or at least you should."

"Meyers, just give me a chance to explain."

"Out!" He jabbed his finger towards the door. Kerri jumped up from the table and headed for the door. She didn't want to get mixed up with a man who could easily have her behind bars. Steve stood his ground and stared hard at the detective.

"I do know you better than this. If you thought there was a way we could solve Len's murder, and maybe Harry's, too, you'd be on board with us instead of fighting us."

"Who? A reporter and a stranger? You expect me to have your back, when you don't have mine?" He quirked a brow. "I saw the paper, Steve. I know that you published information you didn't have authorization to."

"The people of this town have a right to know whether or not they are in danger." Steve's eyes flashed as he looked at Detective Meyers.

Kerri held up her hands. "This was all a

mistake. I'm sorry for that. I'm just going to go."

She opened the door, but Steve pushed it shut. "Wait, I want Detective Meyers to tell us to our faces that he's not going to help solve this murder."

Kerri glared at him and tugged at the handle of the door. "We've upset him enough."

"Wait, wait just a second." Detective Meyers sighed. "You know I'll do what I can. But I'm going to warn both of you right now, this is a situation that could blow up bigger than any of us could imagine. I have no idea who killed Len, the possibilities could range from drug runners to government officials. Is that really something you want to dip your toes into?"

Kerri cringed at the thought.

"All I want is justice. If that's what it takes to get it, then that is fine with me," Steve said.

"I'll be in touch." Detective Meyers shook his head. "But don't do anything stupid. I don't want to find out you've been arrested, understand?"

Kerri nodded. It was the last thing she wanted. Steve opened the door and she hurried through it. As soon as she was on the other side she turned to face him.

"What was that nonsense?"

"What do you mean?"

"I wanted to leave, and you wouldn't let me."

"I didn't want you to give up so easily. I thought we were in this together."

She couldn't hide a slight smile. "Together, huh?"

"If you want to be." He held her gaze. Before she could answer, her grandfather walked down the hall and caught her by the elbow.

"Time to go, Kerri."

"Is everything okay?"

"Just don't make eye contact with anyone, and get to the car."

"What happened?" Steve tried to step between Kerri and George, but George was already tugging her out through the door. Once they were outside, George continued to rush her towards the car. George opened the driver's side and slid in. Kerri settled in the passenger side. Steve opened the back door and got into the car. "No way, you're not going anywhere without some kind of explanation."

George looked in the rearview mirror at him. Then he looked over at Kerri. "We need to get out of here." Kerri frowned as George threw the car into reverse and whipped out of the parking lot. She felt Steve's hand grasp the back of her seat as George took a rather sharp turn.

"What did you do?" Kerri asked. Steve stared back through the rearview mirror. Kerri did her best to avoid looking into his eyes.

"All I did was help myself to a little information that the police were not going to willingly give," George said.

"Like what?" Kerri asked. George turned down a side street.

"Like Len's record. I wanted to know who he

might have been involved in criminal activities with, or whether there were ever any confrontations between Len and Harry, or Chris. Anything that we can get some traction from."

Steve leaned forward from the back seat. "How exactly did you get that information?"

"Never mind that. The important thing is I have it."

"Let's take a look as soon as we can." Kerri tilted her head towards a restaurant down the road. "That looks like as good a place as any."

George looked in the rearview mirror. "Are you sure you want to be part of this? I can drop you off here if you want."

"I'm here, I'm part of it already," Steve said.

"Okay then." George whipped the car into the parking lot of the restaurant. Steve grabbed harder on to the back of Kerri's seat to keep himself steady during the hard turn. She tried not to think about his fingertips as they brushed along her shoulder. A few minutes later they were seated around a table in the Mexican restaurant. George ordered some nachos for the table.

"Let's review it." Kerri tapped the table. "Let's just make sure that no one spots what we have."

"Here you go." George passed her the file beneath a menu. "I haven't had a chance to look at it."

She opened it up and looked at the list of contacts between Len and the police. Her heart dropped as she skimmed over the multiple arrests.

"I'm not so sure that Len was a great guy."

"No, he was a bit of a jerk." Steve frowned. "What's in the file?"

"Six arrests, some for theft, some for dealing in stolen goods," Kerri said.

"Sounds like Len was definitely in the fencing business," Steve said.

"So Detective Meyers was on to something after all." Kerri shook her head. "But why couldn't he prove anything?"

"Maybe Len had someone in his pocket," George suggested. "It wouldn't be the first time that someone evaded prosecution because of influential friends."

"Like Chief Higgins?" Steve asked.

"Maybe." George frowned.

"Well, we know that Len and Frankie the delivery driver were arrested together a few times. So they worked together at one point. Maybe Frankie knew about the money that Len left behind, and decided to try to get to the rest of it. He could have killed Harry in the process," Kerri said.

"I think that's possible." Steve nodded. "I'll let Detective Meyers know about the lead and he might get something more out of Frankie."

"I suppose. What does this mean? Do we think that whoever killed Len also killed Harry? Maybe Frankie crossed both of them?" Kerri suggested.

"Len wasn't going to win any popularity

contests. Harry was a more genial person. He was willing to help his neighbors and generally kept his nose clean. Basically, we have polar opposites. As far as I know Harry didn't have a criminal connection, but he did spend time with both Len and Chris," Steve said.

"But we suspect that Harry knew there was more money stashed in the store. So how did he know?" George asked.

"Maybe Len confided in him before he died." Steve moved his plate aside and glanced out the window.

"Then why would he wait to get the money?" Kerri shook her head. "It wasn't until after we found the money that he volunteered to help me with the floors. I don't think he knew the money was there, but once I found it, I do think that he knew I hadn't found it all. Maybe he knew the amount, but not the hiding place."

"Okay, so he knows the amount. He volunteers to help so he can get the rest of the money. But someone else knew what he was up to," Steve said.

"Chris." George tapped the table. "It's the answer that makes the most sense."

"It is." Steve sat back in his chair. "But, we can't prove it."

"I don't know about Chris. He just doesn't strike me as a murderer." Kerri took a sip of her drink. "I know it's possible, but I think that one of Len's criminal contacts is more likely."

"It's certainly possible," George said.

"What about Delores?" Kerri asked.

"You think Delores killed her husband?" George met her eyes. "That's a rather cruel notion."

"She was so devoted to him. She would always bail him out and was always by his side," Steve said.

"Maybe she was fed up that he was a criminal," Kerri suggested. "She also had the money bands in her pocket."

"But that really doesn't mean anything. Many

banks use the same currency bands. I'm also assuming she deals with the same bank that Len did. They probably use the same paper money bands. Maybe she dipped into their safety deposit box, or their savings, and they used the same bands for the large bills." Steve shrugged. "That's pretty likely."

"Okay, but I know that I've never walked around with currency bands in my pocket." Kerri frowned. "It doesn't make sense to me that she would be."

"She just received a payout for his life insurance." Steve snapped his fingers. "Maybe that's where she got the money."

"You know that for sure?" Kerri met his eyes.

"Yes, I looked into it after Len's death. I mean, if there's a murder, follow the money, right?"

"Isn't that even more motive for her to have killed him?" Kerri asked.

"It could be. It could also be the only good thing her husband did for her."

"So, you really don't think she was involved in his death?"

"No, I don't. I understand why you might think that way, but I've known Delores for some time. I just don't think that she's a killer," Steve said.

"All right, well then we're agreed on Chris as our main suspect?" George brushed some crumbs from his shirt and looked between the two of them.

"I think so." Steve nodded.

"I don't know." Kerri sighed and pushed her plate aside. "I still think that Frankie is a viable suspect. But if that's what you two think, I'm sure it's worth looking into."

"I'll dig up what I can on him. Maybe I can work out what he's been up to recently," Steve said.

"Good idea." George wiped his mouth and signaled to the waitress. "Please let me know what you find out, Steve."

"I will."

"Steve, I don't think that we can rely on Detective Meyers to truly investigate this," Kerri said.

"Give him a little credit, Kerri. I know that things didn't go well today, but he's a good man."

"How do you know that? There are plenty of people that just act like they are a good person. He still didn't give us a good explanation as to why he's so hands off."

"I hear you. I'm not disagreeing, it's just that I've known him for a long time. He's gotten me out of a few sticky situations."

"It seems to me that's the way the police force works here. They do favors and bend the law. That's not exactly something that makes Detective Meyers reliable."

"Sometimes you know a person by their heart, and not so much by their actions."

"I disagree." George took the last swig of his coffee. "I think the only way to truly know someone is by their actions. Even someone with a good heart can engage in horrible actions. It's those actions that define a person."

"Well, then we agree to disagree." Steve shrugged. "When it comes to Detective Meyers, I know that he wouldn't do anything to intentionally harm anyone. Whatever his methods are, his goal is to solve the crime. Otherwise why would he have talked to us? I can tell you that there's a lid on it because of Chief Higgins, not because of Detective Meyers."

"Then maybe we need to look into Chief Higgins. Maybe he's the one that has something to hide," Kerri said.

"Maybe." Steve frowned. "But if you're going to open that can of worms you need to be prepared for the consequences. I can be with you every step of the way."

"Actually, we should get going." George stood up from the table. "Ready, Kerri?"

"Okay." She stood up as well.

"I have to pick up something from the post office so I'll walk back to my car," Steve said.

"Thanks for all of your help." Kerri smiled at Steve.

"No problem. Let me know if you want to brainstorm on this some more."

"I will." She reached for her purse, but he caught her hand in his. She realized as she looked into his eyes that he must have thought she was offering her hand to him. "Thanks again, Steve." As she continued to look into his eyes her heart skipped a beat.

He nodded, gave her hand a light squeeze, then stepped aside so that she could retrieve her purse. As they left the restaurant, her grandfather put his hand lightly on her elbow.

"Careful with that one, Kerri."

"What do you mean?"

"He's awfully interested in all of this."

"He's a reporter. It's his nature to be interested."

"Maybe." He opened the car door for her. "But keep your wits about you."

She studied him for a moment, then nodded. On the drive back to the house she thought about her grandfather's concern. Could he be right about Steve? He had a lot more experience with reading people than she did. That was why she had acquiesced to the idea of Chris being the main suspect. Surely a reporter and a spy would know a killer when they saw one. Maybe seeing Chris with Harry's family had distorted her ability to remain impartial towards him. Either way she had to stay focused on getting her store open. She had too much on the line to let everything fall apart.

Chapter Twelve

After Kerri and George arrived at the house, Kerri hooked Cashew up to her leash and took her out back to get some air. She released her in an area that she knew was safe. As she watched her scamper and play she smiled with pride. Cashew had been a constant part of her life for a very long time. When Cashew disappeared into the woods that lined the property she chased after her.

"Cashew! Cashew, come back here!" She ran into the woods behind her. Cashew ran faster, until she reached a fallen tree and skidded to a stop. She sat down, and looked at the tree, but did not bark.

"What is it, Cash? What caught your eye?" She crouched down beside her pet. After she snapped on her leash, she looked towards the tree. Perched there, with wide eyes and a rigid tail, was a very familiar squirrel.

"Hi there." She smiled at him. "Do you want

to show me your home?" The squirrel bobbed his head up and down as if he might be nodding. "I think I might have some nuts in my purse." She felt around for a small bag of nuts she had tucked away, and opened the bag. Then she scattered them on the ground for the squirrel. The squirrel dashed forward to collect them. "What I wouldn't give to have your eyes and ears little fellow. I imagine that you always know who to trust and who to be frightened of, not like we humans that can't seem to figure it out."

The squirrel fluffed its tail and puffed out its cheeks. "Yes, someone is always putting on a show."

Kerri crouched down and rocked back on her heels as she looked up at the sky. It was a gorgeous place to live. But was a potentially corrupt town really where she wanted to start a business? She thought back to her years in boarding school. Even though she was surrounded by other girls her age she didn't make friends easily. She was always planning for the future. Now that the future was here, she wondered if she'd gone in the wrong direction. "Well, pal, I've got to be going. I hope we can talk again soon." She wiggled her fingers at the squirrel. He flicked his tail at her. Cashew trotted up to her and licked her palm to see if there were any nuts left. Amazed by how docile Cashew was around the squirrel, she looked into her eyes.

"You know a friend when you see one, too, don't you, Cash?" She stroked her ears and smiled. When she stepped back into the house her grandfather had some papers spread across the table.

"What are you up to, Grandpa?"

He froze when she walked into the kitchen. "Oh, I thought you went out for a while."

"No, I just took Cashew out back. Why?" She folded her arms and raised an eyebrow. "Is there something you don't want me to see?"

He hesitated and fluttered through the papers before looking back up at her. "I suppose it's too late to keep it a secret now."

"You shouldn't need to keep it a secret."

"Look, Kerri, whoever killed Harry did so in your shop. To me that means that the murder needs to be solved quickly."

"I agree with that." She shrugged and looked down at the papers. They appeared to be a blueprint of a house. "What is this for?"

"This is Harry's house. I want to get in and take a look around."

"You really want to break into the murder victim's house?" Her eyes widened. "I thought you had decided against it when you didn't mention it again."

"I just wanted to pick the right time."

"That doesn't seem like a very good idea."

"It is, if I know exactly how to get in and out."

"How are you going to know how to do that?" She frowned.

"See this." He tapped the blueprint. "This shows me all of the entrances and exits of the house. Based on experience I can predict the easiest way in and out. I'll be able to get in, and get back out, in just a few minutes."

"Grandpa, that is a crime, too. What if we get caught?"

"What do you mean, we?" He met her eyes. "This is something that I'm doing."

"Not alone you're not. If you want to risk your freedom to protect my shop, and me, then I'm going to risk my freedom, too."

"You don't see how that defeats the purpose of me protecting you?"

"Maybe I want to protect you, too."

His expression softened as he smiled. "That means a lot to me, Kerri."

"I guess we're in this together then. When are we going?"

"Tonight would be the best time, before any evidence is removed or inadvertently lost."

"Won't we be contaminating a crime scene?"

"Not really. The crime took place at your shop.

The police have had their chance to search Harry's house for any evidence. We're just taking a second look. Helping out the police really."

"I'm sure." She smiled. "Okay, tonight. Do I need to dress in black?"

"It doesn't hurt to wear darker clothing, but only in a casual way. The last thing you want is for someone to spot you in head to toe black clothes, they're sure to be suspicious of that."

"Good advice." She glanced at her watch. "What time?"

"Nine o'clock. Late enough that everyone is inside, early enough that a little noise won't draw attention."

"Wow, you really do have experience with this kind of thing. Is this the kind of thing that you would do before you retired?"

His lips tightened and he shook his head. "I can't really talk about that."

"Okay." She studied him for a moment. What was her grandfather's life really like? Her only concept of spies came from the movies and she was sure that wasn't very accurate. "I do hope that one day you'll trust me enough to share some of what you have experienced."

He looked up at her and held her gaze. "It's not about trust, Kerri. Some things I'd rather not remember, and others it's in my best interest not to mention. Aside from that, I want to be your grandfather, Kerri. The man I was at work isn't who I am now. Can you understand that?"

She bit into her bottom lip but nodded. He placed a hand on her shoulder and rubbed it.

"I know this is all a little confusing for you, Kerri. There's so much that we've missed out on. But now we can make up for that."

"By breaking into a house."

"By solving a crime."

"Nine o'clock it is. I'll just get changed." She hurried off to her room in an attempt to hide her frustration. There were so many things she wanted to know, so many things she was curious about, but her grandfather still had a right to his privacy. That was something that she was going to have to accept, even if she didn't like it. She changed into casual, dark clothes and wondered if she was getting caught up in something out of her element. Her grandfather was right, she might be more of a liability by tagging along. But she couldn't let him get involved without her. It was her store after all. When she turned to leave her room she heard a chatter at the window. She turned to find the squirrel on her windowsill. The glass windowpanes between them drowned out some of his chattering, but he was insistent on wanting her attention. The squirrel was friendly, but did she want to risk him chewing through the screen and getting into her room? The squirrel chattered again. She sighed and opened the window.

"What are you doing, silly billy? You're supposed to be at your tree not on my windowsill." He stopped chattering and looked into her eyes. She noticed that he had something wrapped around his paw. As she looked closer, the squirrel was spooked and ran. The shred of paper was left on her windowsill. It was a piece of the same money bands that she found in her shop. "Now, where did you get that?" She picked up her purse and discovered that she was missing some of the bands that she'd tucked in there. Maybe she'd somehow dropped them on the way into the house from the car. Maybe they'd fallen out when she chased after the squirrel or took the nuts out of her bag. He brought it back to her. There was no other possible solution. It wasn't as if the squirrel could be directing her where to look in the case. She was a rational person. Squirrels didn't solve murders. But the more she thought about it, the more she thought the squirrel might be right.

If the money was what connected the murders, then she needed to find out more about it. Her best resource for that was going to be Chris, Len's brother and business partner. He had to know where all the money came from. She paused in front of her mirror and added a little makeup. With her lips plumped, and her hair fluffed, she slipped out the front door. She didn't want her grandfather to know what she was up to just yet.

Kerri drove past Harry's parents' house to check if Chris was there. When she didn't see his car she pulled over to the side of the road and contemplated her next steps. Chris had just flown into town. He could be registered at a hotel or staying with friends. She had no idea how to find out which was the case. She decided she needed a little help. Even though her grandfather had warned her against trusting him, she called Steve's number.

"Hi, Kerri, I'm glad you called. Any news?"

"Not just yet. Do you think you could help me with something?"

"Name it."

"I want to find out where Chris is staying."

"Why?"

"I just need to know. Can you help me find out where he is staying please?"

"Yes, I can. In fact, I already know where he's staying. But why do you want to know?"

"I have my reasons."

"What's with all the secrecy? Are you afraid I'm going to publish your plans?"

"I want to talk with Chris, but I want to talk with him by myself. I think he'll be more likely to talk freely if it's just me there."

"Okay, that's a good plan. Just keep me on speed dial in case you get into any trouble."

"Really? You're not going to try to talk me out of it?"

"No. I don't think that Chris will do anything rash, but if he does I'm sure you can handle it. Call me if you need anything."

"I will." She smiled. It was nice not to be treated as if she wasn't capable. "So where is he staying?"

"At Vuebelle Hotel just outside of town. He's

in room 109."

"How do you know that?"

"I've been keeping track of him since he came back into the area. You're right, I didn't get much out of him. Maybe you will. Let me know, all right?"

"Sure. I will. Thanks for your help." She hung up the phone and entered the name of the hotel into her GPS. It was one of the few higher end hotels in the area. If he was staying there then it didn't appear as if money was much of an issue for him. But why was he staying there instead of with his sister-in-law? Perhaps they'd had a falling out, too.

Chapter Thirteen

Kerri parked not far from the entrance of the hotel and walked up the sidewalk to the door. As she rode the elevator to the second floor it occurred to her that she didn't have any kind of plan. She looked nice enough, but that wasn't going to get her in the door. What would she say to Chris when he answered? What if he didn't answer? Her heart pounded as she walked down the hall to room 109. When she paused outside it she considered going back home without ever knocking. However, the thought of having to admit to Steve that she didn't follow through motivated her to knock on the door. After the second knock the door swung open. Chris smiled the moment he saw her.

"I remember you."

"You do?" She swallowed hard. Their last interaction had been full of tension.

"Sure. I met you at Harry's folks' house. Isn't

that right?"

"Yes."

He rested his shoulder against the doorway and raked his gaze from the top of her head to the tips of her toes before he looked back into her eyes again. "Want to come in?"

Her stomach twisted for a moment. What if he was the killer? Should she go into his hotel room alone? She felt like Chris was testing her. If she refused to go in, he would assume she didn't trust him. If she wanted to get any information from him, she had to go into the room. She forced a smile.

"Yes, I would love that."

"Great. I just ordered some wine." He stepped aside so that she could move past him. Kerri braced herself as she stepped over the threshold.

"Drinking alone?"

"Not anymore." He smiled as he poured two glasses. The only place to sit was a small couch not far from the bed. She accepted the glass of wine and sat down on the couch. He sat down beside her, so close that his knee brushed hers. "So why are you here? Kerri, right?"

"Honestly, I'm here because I'm curious."

"Oh?" He took a sip of his wine. "Curious about what?"

"I bought this shop, at a great deal, and I thought that I was getting ready to start my future. You know?"

"And then, Harry ended up dead."

"It's not just that. When I bought it I had no idea that the former owner, your brother, was murdered." She sighed and stared down into her glass of wine. "I just can't help but wonder if I'm even safe in that shop. Should I even try to open it, or is disaster going to strike again?"

"So, you came to ask me if you're in danger?" He shifted a little closer to her on the couch. "And not drink my wine?"

"I'm sorry, I'm just scared." Her eyes widened as she looked into his. "I thought maybe you would know what someone might have been looking for in the shop. I mean, I knew that Len was up to something. I found all of that money under the floor. I just thought that you could give me an idea of what I'm up against. Drugs? Mafia? Angry mistress?"

"No small talk with you, huh?" He took another swig of his wine. "I do appreciate your honesty. I'll try to offer you the same. Sure, my brother was involved in something less than legal. No, I'm not going to tell you what it was because it could potentially implicate me as well. But it didn't have to do with drugs or the mafia."

"So, he was just fencing?"

He coughed on his next sip of wine. "Who told you that?"

"Frankie." She locked eyes with him.

"I don't believe that. Frankie would never tell you anything. Besides he and my brother weren't working together anymore. Frankie wanted nothing to do with him. He turned his life around. He started a business."

"So, Len was involved in fencing?"

"You're putting words in my mouth."

"I'm just trying to find out what happened. What about the money? Who knew about it other than you?"

"I didn't even know about the money."

"So, you just happened to show up in town right around the time Harry was killed?" She stared hard into his eyes.

"Don't you think that if I knew that there was money hidden in that shop I would have taken it before you ever bought it? Why would I take the risk that you would find it? I can't believe you turned it in to the police by the way. How foolish."

"It's not foolish, it's the right thing to do. I have no interest in keeping illegal money."

"Aren't you refreshing?" He set his glass of wine down and eyed hers. "Are you going to drink that?"

"So, you didn't know about the money being hidden in the store. Why did you come back?"

176

"I come back at least every few weeks." He shrugged. "You can check that, right? Or have your friend do it for you? It was just a coincidence that Harry was killed on the same day."

"Then where were you when he was killed?"

Chris reached out and took her glass of wine from her hand. After a long sip of it he smiled.

"I was with someone who was willing to drink my wine. She prefers not to be named, and I won't be telling anyone my business. But I was with her all morning and well into the afternoon."

"And I suppose your lady friend would like to keep it a secret, too."

"She would. Let's just say, we prefer our privacy. Anyway, I don't think you have anything to be concerned about. If this was about the money, well the money is gone now."

"I guess you're right. Thanks for the reassurance."

"Good luck with the new shop. Just be aware that this town has its secrets, and the sooner you decide not to look into them, the better off you will be."

Kerri stood up and offered him her hand. "Thanks for your time, Chris."

He grasped it, and held it a little longer than was comfortable. When she tugged her hand free, he smiled at her.

"Whenever you want to share a glass of wine, you let me know."

As Kerri stepped out of the hotel room her skin crawled. If he was in town to see his girlfriend why was he being so flirtatious with her? She turned to walk down the hall and nearly walked into someone who leaned against the wall beside the door.

"Steve! What are you doing here?"

"What were you doing in his hotel room?" He caught her by the arm and steered her off into the nearby stairwell.

"I told you I was coming to see Chris."

"Yes, but you didn't tell me you intended to go

into his hotel room alone. What sense does that make? I thought you would use more caution than that." He met her eyes with a frown. "He might be a murderer, Kerri, and you were in the room alone with him?"

"I can handle myself." She crossed her arms.

"The only reason you're still alive is because Chris didn't want you dead."

"That's a little extreme. If I hadn't gone in, he wouldn't have told me anything."

"And did you find out anything?" He searched her eyes.

"I found out that he has an alibi. Which means he's not our murderer, even though you and my grandfather think he is. Also, Frankie wasn't working with Len at the time of Len's death. Still, maybe he had a bone to pick with him."

"Wait, what alibi does Chris have?" He matched her pace as she started down the stairs.

"He was with a woman at the time of the murder."

"Who?"

"I don't know. He wouldn't tell me."

"Then how is it an alibi?" He shook his head as they reached the bottom of the stairs. "He could have been making it up."

"He wasn't."

"How do you know?" He opened the door for her. She stepped through and looked over at him.

"I know. I just do."

"Sounds to me like he was trying to convince you to throw the suspicion off himself."

"Well, then I guess we'll have to find out who the woman is. Let's ask the staff if they've ever noticed him here with a woman," Kerri suggested as she walked towards the front desk.

"I doubt that they'll tell us that."

"I guess you're right." Kerri turned away from the front desk and started to walk away. Steve trailed after her.

"That's it? You're just going to give up."

"What else can I do?"

"We can get a look at those cameras," Steve said as he looked towards the front desk. Kerri followed Steve's gaze and noticed the bank of monitors that played the footage from the security cameras.

"How?"

"We just need to create a distraction that will draw the clerk away from the desk. Then I can roll back the cameras to the time of Harry's death and see if Chris really was meeting with someone," Steve said.

"Okay, I guess it's worth a shot. But what kind of distraction?"

"Maybe a fight, that always works in the movies. Is Natalie free?"

"She might be. I'll call her."

As Kerri called Natalie, Steve filled her in on his plan. "When she arrives pick a fight with her, as if she's someone that has been seeing your husband. If you make it believable enough the woman behind the counter will try to escort you both out."

She cringed at the thought, but nodded. When Natalie picked up she filled her in on the plan. Natalie agreed.

"She'll be here in ten minutes."

"Okay, I'm going to hang out near the counter so I'll be able to get to the cameras. Make it look good, Kerri."

"I'll try, but I'm not a very confrontational person."

He grinned at her. "You could have fooled me. I showed a little concern, and you nearly took my head off."

"There's no harm in taking a few risks to get to the truth."

His smile lingered as he studied her. "Yes, but you're much too wonderful to risk."

She blinked at his words. Her cheeks warmed, and she got a bit tongue-tied. He winked at her and walked away. While she was still trying to work out what his comment meant, Natalie sent a text to say that she was outside the hotel.

Kerri took a deep breath and tried to think back to moments when she'd been furious. There weren't many. She usually got along pretty well with just about everyone that she met. Once in the eighth grade an older girl got the idea that Kerri was flirting with her boyfriend. Then she'd spread a rumor through the whole school that she was an orphan, and that was why she was at boarding school. It went on for a few days before Kerri got fed up enough to confront the girl. Even then she'd given her a chance to explain. However, the girl was not as kind and had taken a swing at her. Kerri didn't hesitate to hit her back. It was that sensation that she tried to summon up from deep within her when Natalie walked through the door.

"You! I knew it was you!" She stepped in front of Natalie and didn't let her get a step closer to the desk. "How could you do this to me?"

Natalie stared at her with wide eyes. "You must be confused. I have no idea what you're talking about."

"I'm talking about Tom! He's my husband and he loves me, and you know it!"

"Is that what you think?" She laughed right in her friend's face. "If he's with you then why did he invite me here?"

"Because you seduced him! You took a good man and you turned him bad!"

"He just doesn't want what you're offering!" Natalie fluffed her hair. "Plenty of men prefer a little meat on a woman's bones."

"You homewrecker!" Kerri lunged forward. The clerk rounded the desk and ran straight towards them.

"None of that! If you two don't leave right this second I will call the police."

"Go ahead and call them!" Kerri shoved her hands against Natalie's shoulders. Natalie gasped and stumbled back. Kerri realized that her friend hadn't been expecting that.

"That's it, I'm calling security and the police!"

The clerk pulled out her cell phone and began to dial. Kerri knew that she had to keep her attention long enough for Steve to get the information that he needed.

"What's wrong? You can't defend yourself? You know why? Because you're wrong. You're a terrible person who is trying to steal my husband from me and our twins!"

"Ha! Maybe if you did something to satisfy him at home he wouldn't have to wander. You're the only one that's to blame." Natalie punched Kerri on the side of her arm with a force that was no more than a tap. But Kerri took the opportunity to collapse to the floor and writhe in pain.

"Ow! Ow! Look what she did! I'm going to press charges!" It occurred to Kerri that actual police might arrive soon. She glanced over at the front desk and saw Steve crouched behind it. She continued to writhe on the floor in pain.

"Oh no! Look what you did to her?" The clerk shouted at Natalie. Natalie gasped.

"I barely hit her! I don't know!" Natalie exclaimed. "Are you okay?" Natalie crouched down next to her. Kerri glanced over Natalie's shoulder and saw Steve nod from behind the counter indicating that he had what he needed.

Slowly she sat up and looked at Natalie, then the clerk.

"Where am I?"

"You're at the Vuebelle Hotel." The clerk pursed her lips. "You know just where you are."

"No, I don't. I'm sorry. What happened? I must have forgotten my medication this morning. Sometimes I get a little disoriented."

Kerri held her hand up to the clerk. The clerk took it, and Kerri pulled her towards her enough that Steve was able to crawl out from behind the front desk. Once Kerri was on her feet she turned towards Natalie.

"Don't worry about it, you can keep him." As she walked out of the front door she picked up a napkin stamped with the hotel's name and address that was next to some complimentary pastries. She used it to dab at her eyes. She met Natalie around the corner from the hotel.

"Kerri, good acting. I didn't really hurt you did I?" She looked at her friend.

"No, I'm sorry if I went overboard. I just didn't want Steve to get caught. We're trying to make sure that Chris actually has an alibi and figure out who he was with on the day that Harry was killed."

"And, I did." Steve jogged up to both of them. "Kerri, that was an amazing performance."

"It seemed to work." She glanced down the road. "We need to get out of here before the police show up."

"Okay, let's duck into the café. It's pretty busy in there, I doubt that the police will spot us," Steve said.

"I hope not," Kerri said.

Chapter Fourteen

Steve led Kerri and Natalie into the nearby café and asked to sit at the counter. Once they were settled at the counter, Kerri turned towards Steve.

"All right, so what did you find?"

"Unfortunately, not everything we wanted. I did find that there was a woman who left his room late in the afternoon. However, I couldn't get any footage of when she entered the room. So, we don't know whether he was actually occupied during the exact time of Harry's murder."

"What about the woman? We can ask her can't we? She should be able to give us a timeline."

"That's the other problem. I couldn't get a good view of her face. I have no idea who she is."

"Great. So we did all of this for nothing."

"Not for nothing. We now know that Chris was telling the truth. He was here meeting with a woman. If he came here to meet with her, then she might be a local or at least from nearby. If she's from around here, then I probably know who she is, I've probably seen her and talked with her. There's no one in this town that I haven't. This is a piece, and I will be able to fit it into the puzzle."

"That's very confident of you, Steve, but what if it isn't him? Then who is left for us to suspect?"

He shook his head as he slid his hands into his pockets. "I can't tell you that. My hunch is still pinned on Chris."

"Chris may be a lot of things, but he's never done anything to hurt anyone." Natalie frowned. "I can't picture him killing his own brother."

Kerri felt some relief at her friend's support. She didn't want to be the only one that didn't suspect Chris.

"Classic motive. Sibling rivalry, money problems, loyalty issues. Everything is there," Steve said.

"Just because it's classic doesn't mean that it's true." Kerri sighed and stood up from the counter.

"I need to get back to the house. Just let me know if you track anyone down that you think might be Chris' secret lover."

"Secret lover." He chuckled. "Okay, I'll do that." Heat billowed up through Kerri as she locked eyes with him. As helpful as he was, there were moments when she thought he simply found her amusing.

"Thanks, Steve."

As Kerri left the café, Natalie followed after her. "What is up between the two of you?"

"Nothing. He's just helping me try to figure things out."

"It doesn't feel like nothing to me."

"Natalie, please." She flashed a smile at her friend. "I have bigger concerns right now. Like that police car in the hotel parking lot."

"Ouch. Yes, I guess we didn't think that part through. Want a lift home?"

"That would be great. I can pick up my car later."

"And, the ride will give us some time to dish."

"Natalie."

"Kerri." She grinned at her. "I parked over here." She pointed to the gas station beside the hotel. "I figured if we were going to be going covert I should be a bit more careful."

"Wiser than me." Kerri walked beside her towards the car. Natalie hit the remote on her keys to unlock the door. As Kerri got inside she looked across the top of the car to the hotel. "What if we're wrong, Natalie? What if it is Chris? Do you think I just put a target on my back?"

"I think that you need to clear your mind, and focus on something else for a little while. Anytime I fixate on something I can't figure it out until I manage to forget about it."

"That's an interesting method." She smiled as she sat down in the car. "I can't say I've tried it."

"Trust me, it works. Do something to relax, and let go a little. It gives your brain some time to stretch."

"But how can you not focus on it when something is so important?"

"It takes a little practice. One good way would be to talk to me about that sizzle between you and Steve."

"Sizzle?" Kerri pretended that her ears weren't burning. "I don't know what you mean."

"Sure you do. He's hot, there's no getting around that. But like I said, he's a powder keg. Some women like that kind of man I guess."

"Not me!" Kerri shook her head, then closed her eyes for a moment. "My last boyfriend took me to the library where we met for our anniversary. That's not exactly risky behavior."

"And he's not exactly your boyfriend anymore. Is he?" Natalie tilted her head to the side and smiled.

Kerri opened her mouth to defend herself but realized she couldn't. Ethan was amazing to her, and yet she'd walked away from him because something was missing. Was it that he was just too good? There was no denying that Steve made her heart pound every time she was near him.

"I've got too much going on right now to even consider it, Natalie. Besides, he hasn't exactly shown any interest. The only reason we're even talking is because there's a murder to solve. That doesn't sound very romantic does it?"

Natalie laughed. "You've got me there. It's not a common way to ignite a relationship." She pulled into Kerri's driveway and parked. "Do you want me to come in and brainstorm with you?"

Kerri glanced at her watch. It was after seven and she guessed that her grandfather was preparing for the break-in. She didn't want Natalie finding out about it.

"No, that's okay. We can regroup in the morning. I think I need to put some ice on that bruise that you left."

"Bruise?" Her eyes widened. Kerri smiled.

"I'm just kidding. You barely touched me."

"Good." She sighed with relief. "I'm a lover

not a fighter. Although, I think we're going to get a lot of laughs out of this experience in the years to come."

"I like the sound of that." Kerri grinned as she got out of the car. It meant a lot to her that their friendship might last for years. That was if she ever got her store off the ground. She opened the door to the house and found her grandfather in the front hallway. He crossed his arms the moment she stepped inside.

"You could have told me what you were up to."

"How did you know?" She stared at him.

"I have my ways."

"This is ridiculous." She tossed her purse down on a side table and studied him. "I am not five, Grandpa. I don't need to be monitored."

"I know that." He relaxed his arms and smiled a little. "But you still could have told me. You may be strong, intelligent, and capable, but that doesn't mean you don't need someone that you can trust. I told you about the break-in, didn't I?"

"Yes." She sighed.

"Then why not tell me about your plan?"

"I didn't want to offend you I guess."

"How would you have offended me?" His brow furrowed.

"Because I wanted to speak to him alone. I went there to try to prove that Chris didn't do it, not to prove that he did. I know that you and Steve think he is probably the killer, but I don't. I thought maybe if we could take the focus off him then we might be able to make some actual progress on working out who the murderer is."

"Fair enough. Don't ever think that you have to agree with me. You have a sharp mind, and if you think that I'm wrong you're more than welcome to voice that opinion. You're right about not needing to be monitored. We're partners in this. Okay?" He held his hand out to her. She smiled with relief and took it in hers.

"Partners." She nodded.

"Let's go over the plan one more time before we head out."

"Perfect." She followed him into the kitchen. For the next hour they spent time looking over the blueprints and discussing what areas of the house to pay the most attention to.

When they were finished George drove her back to the hotel to pick up her car. She was relieved to find that there was no staff or police in sight when she picked it up.

When Kerri dropped her car back at the house she quickly went inside before they left for their clandestine adventure. Kerri made sure that Cashew had plenty of water and a little extra food. She didn't mention to her grandfather why, but in the back of her mind she was concerned that they wouldn't make it home. What if they were arrested and no one was able to feed Cashew until the next day? She gave her an extra pat and snuggle before following her grandfather out the door.

Chapter Fifteen

The drive to Harry's house was a quiet one. Kerri was afraid that if she spoke, she might change her mind about the entire thing. Her grandfather stared hard through the windshield as if he might be searching for something that wasn't visible on the road. Once more she wondered about his life. Now that she knew more about him, her entire perspective had shifted. The man she'd once considered a strange but fascinating person had morphed into a genuine mystery. Kerri now understood the things he insisted she learn with him. He'd given her enough education to know how to protect herself, and what to do in dangerous situations.

"We'll park here so that we won't raise any suspicions. That means that if we need to run for it, we're going to have to really sprint." He glanced down at her shoes and nodded. "You should be fine."

"What if we are caught?" She froze with her

hand on the door handle. "What are we going to do?"

"You're going to say that you were looking for me, and that you had no idea what I was up to." He locked eyes with her. "Understand?"

"Grandpa, that's not right. I can't let you take the fall."

"You're not letting me do anything. I know how to deal with the authorities, you do not. One of us needs to be free, and I'd prefer that it be you. All right?" She nodded and started to open the door. He grabbed her by the elbow. "Don't worry, we're not going to get caught."

Kerri's stomach churned. She wanted to believe him, but she wasn't convinced. As she stepped out of the car he walked around the front and gestured for her to follow right behind him. They moved through the shadows of the sides of houses until they made it to the kitchen door of Harry's house. It was dark like she expected it to be. It was a small house, about the size of a cottage, and the backyard was littered with remnants of Harry's handyman jobs. Vines grew up through an old, broken toilet. A pile of salvaged wood leaned up against the back of the house.

"We're in." George pushed the door open. Kerri's breath grew shallow. This was it, the moment she would cross the line, and become a criminal. She stepped in behind her grandfather and went straight for the kitchen drawers. Her grandfather began to rummage through the living room. She found pushpins, silverware, and an assortment of matchbooks. On a scratch pad several addresses were written down along with the job that was supposed to be done at the address. She noticed that he'd listed Len's house, and noted that he needed to repair a door and a window. She snapped a picture of the note, then moved on to another drawer. Inside she found a variety of take-out food menus and small packets of sauces. She began to get discouraged. There didn't seem to be any clues to find.

When Kerri opened the last drawer she discovered there was a small disposable cell phone tucked inside. She flipped it open and tried to turn it on. It flashed then displayed a screen. She scrolled down through the recent calls and discovered that there were quite a few calls to the same number. She took a photo of the number so she could follow up on it later. A few minutes into the search her grandfather stepped into the kitchen with something in his hand.

"Look at this." He held up an envelope and opened the flap. "Quite a bit of cash to be stashed here, don't you think?"

"Yes." She stared at the envelope. "Is there a letter inside explaining where it came from."

"No. But there is something on the back here." He turned the envelope over and displayed a smudged stamp on the back. "It's hard to make out but there's a partial address."

"Did you find anything else?"

"Just this." He held up a file. "I think it means something. It was hidden with the envelope in the balustrade. Easy for the police to miss the little piece of wood that could be pulled away. If we can't work it out, maybe Steve will have a look at it."

"We should leave the money here. But let's snap a picture of the stamp on the back of the envelope."

"And this?" George held up the file.

"Bring it. I doubt that anyone is going to miss that."

"Okay, let's get out of here before our luck runs out."

Kerri used her cell phone to take a picture of the envelope, then tucked it away. "Let's go." She peeked through the front window to be sure that the road out front was clear. "It looks good."

He opened the door and stepped out, then waved her through. As she stepped outside into the dark, she wondered at how her life had changed. She had never broken into someone's house in the middle of the night before. But there she was, sneaking her way down the front walkway to the car with her grandfather right behind her. She opened the door to the car, and her grandfather rushed around the car to the driver's side. As soon as she was inside he started the car and steered it down the road at a speed that wouldn't draw too much attention.

"That's it, we're in the clear." George smiled.

"Why doesn't it feel like that then? My heart is racing." She held her hands together so tight that her fingers ached. At every turn she expected a police car to come speeding up behind them. "We shouldn't have done that. What was I thinking?"

"Relax, Kerri. It's over. We got what we needed, and hopefully we'll be able to work out some things. Don't worry so much. I'm not going to let you go to jail."

"You're not going to let me go to jail? Somehow you think there's a way to prevent that?"

"I know there's a way." He winked at her. "Your old Grandpa has still got some tricks up his sleeve."

She studied him for a moment. As strange as it was to think of him as a spy, she could see it in his expression, in his confidence. He was his own person, who had lived his own adventures.

"You're not old." She sighed. "Not even a little."

"I know." He looked over at her. "There's a lot we're going to have to learn about each other, Kerri. I just hope that's something you want to do."

"It is." She managed a smile as he turned the car down the driveway to her house. However, Kerri's smile vanished when the headlights revealed that another car, aside from hers, was parked in the driveway. The light on the dash gave away that it was an unmarked police car. Her stomach lurched. "I sure hope you have a few tricks, Grandpa, because it looks like we've been caught."

"Just relax. Stay calm. They don't know anything if we don't say anything. Understand?"

Her chest tightened as she saw Detective

Meyers step out of the car. For a moment panic seized her. She thought about telling her grandfather to throw the car into reverse and drive as far and fast as he could in the other direction. However, Detective Meyers had the entire police department at his disposal and she was certain that he could easily catch up with them. Besides that, her grandfather had already opened the door and was stepping out of the car.

"Is there a problem, Detective?" He crossed his arms. Kerri made her way out of the passenger side and tried to keep her nerves under control so she wouldn't faint. She hung by the car as Detective Meyers stepped towards both of them.

"It's a bit late to be out and about isn't it?"

"Is there some kind of curfew I didn't know about?" George met his eyes.

"No curfew, but I like to think that the good people in town keep to themselves after a certain hour. They don't go around breaking into houses." That was it, she was going to faint. She turned away to try to calm down, but Detective Meyers put a hand on her shoulder. "Why are you getting yourself wrapped up in all of this, Kerri?"

Kerri cleared her throat. She had the feeling that Detective Meyers was honing in on her because he thought she was the weak link.

"I don't know what you're talking about. We just went for a drive to look for places for my grandfather to live."

"Oh?" He chuckled. "So the two people spotted going in and out of Harry's house, weren't you two?"

Her stomach clenched. "No. I have no idea what you're talking about."

"Why don't you ask me, if you want to know something, Detective?" George stepped in front of her. "If you want to accuse someone of something, it should be me."

Detective Meyers gazed at him. "Cut the tough guy act. You know you got her involved in something you shouldn't have. If I had any solid proof I would have every right to arrest both of you right this second."

Kerri closed her eyes and willed herself not to cry. Her grandfather remained in front of her.

"That's right you have no proof. So stop with the threats, you're scaring Kerri," George said.

"Why shouldn't I? She needs to be scared. She could have been shot breaking into someone's house. Maybe the only way to protect her from you is to put her in handcuffs."

"She doesn't need to be protected from me."

"Oh yeah? I looked into you. You have a record."

"That was a misunderstanding and was supposed to be expunged." George crossed his arms. "Maybe you should look into me a little more."

"Is that supposed to be a threat?" He chuckled and shook his head. "I don't know what the two of you think, but this is not a town for criminals."

"It isn't?" Kerri moved boldly in front of her grandfather. "Because from what I can tell the police don't seem to be too interested in solving crime. Maybe I have the wrong impression, but I don't think that's the case."

"You're wrong, young lady. Which is why I'm here." She held her breath as she prepared for him to grab her by the wrists and thrust her into the car. Instead, he took off his hat and looked at both of them. "You need to be careful. So, is there any information that you want to share with me about the murders?"

"That's interesting. If the police investigated this murder properly why would you want to know what information we have?" Kerri asked.

"Because, I want to know if you found anything that points to anyone as a suspect?"

Before Kerri could answer her grandfather spoke up for her. "Why should we tell you anything?"

"Because I'm doing what I can. I'm trying to solve a murder. So, if you know anything important about the murder you should tell me."

"We don't know anything that can help." George stared hard at him. "Now, if you'll excuse us, it's late."

The detective reluctantly nodded. "If there's anything that might help the case, I'd like to be informed."

"Sure." Kerri moved past him and her grandfather towards the door. "We'll let you know."

Detective Meyers gripped his hat and opened his mouth as if he might have something more to say. Instead he nodded to them again and headed back to his car. Kerri unlocked the door and left it open for her grandfather to step in behind her. As soon as they were inside, the detective's car pulled out of the driveway. George leaned back against the door and sighed. "Well, that was close."

"Yes. And strange. He suspected that we might have been in Harry's house and all he wanted was information? What kind of detective is that?"

"The kind that just might have a guilty

conscience. We need to keep an eye on him."

"Yes, I think so, too. His behavior is very suspicious."

"That it is. Why don't we take a look at the file?" He tossed it down on the kitchen table.

"I also found a cell phone of Harry's. It was charged, it turned on, and there were several calls to the same number." She held up her phone to show him the photo she had taken of the number.

"Let me take a look." He picked up her phone and looked at the number. Kerri flipped open the file and was greeted by photographs of a door and a window.

"Why did you take this, Grandpa? They look like work photographs."

"There's a note on the inside of the file that made me think differently." He grabbed his own phone and began to punch in numbers.

"What are you doing?"

"I'm going to see who Harry was calling." As he waited on the phone, she read over the note on the inside of the file.

"Sunday nine PM." She frowned. "That's rather late to be doing a job."

"And on the weekend." George nodded then held up a finger. He listened for a moment, then hung up the phone. "It went to an automated voicemail. No idea who it belongs to."

"Maybe we can have Steve look it up."

"Maybe." He brushed his hand along his chin and looked over at the file.

"Look, I still think these pictures might be for a job. It was at Len's house, after the break-in. See?" She showed him the snapshot of the address and duties that Harry jotted down on the notebook. "He was supposed to repair a door, and a window. Those are probably pictures of the damage. I remember him talking to the locksmith about it."

"Interesting. So he went to Delores' house Sunday at nine o'clock at night to fix it? Or maybe that's when the pictures were taken?"

"Maybe." Kerri rubbed her eyes. Her head ached from trying to force the pieces together. In that moment she remembered what Natalie had told her. "I think we need to sleep on it. We can look at all of this again in the morning."

"All right." He closed the folder and set his phone on top of it. "Good night, Kerri."

"Good night, Grandpa."

She carried Cashew into her room with her and closed the door. The moment she stretched out on the bed, Cashew snuggled up beside her. As her eyes fell closed she smiled at the memory of Steve's touch. Just as Natalie suspected, she was starting to feel something for him. As curious as she was about him she was fairly certain that Steve didn't feel the same way. She was a gateway to a big story for him, and nothing more than that. She fell asleep with Cashew's nose nuzzled up against her cheek.

Chapter Sixteen

The insistent ring of her cell phone summoned Kerri out of what could have been a good dream. She opened her eyes and looked towards her phone. Cashew was curled up on her belly, making it impossible to get up. She stretched her fingers as far as they would go and managed to grasp the phone. When she saw it was Steve she answered it.

"Hello?" Her cheeks flushed at how rough her voice was first thing in the morning.

"Kerri, are you okay?"

She cleared her throat. "Yes, sorry. Just waking up."

"Oh, I hadn't thought about that. I'm sorry. I'm usually up by five, and six-thirty seems a bit late to me."

"What's up, Steve?"

"Would you like to go to breakfast with me?"

"Breakfast? Now?"

"Yes. I mean, if you're not going back to sleep."

"Okay." She managed to wriggle out from under Cashew. "But why?"

"I know yesterday I was a little short with you."

"That's okay."

"I just didn't want you to get hurt. Anyway, I've done some research and I have an idea of who Chris might have been meeting with at the hotel. So, are you going to share some breakfast with me to find out?"

She smiled and walked over to her closet. "Absolutely. I'll need about thirty minutes."

"Okay, I'll pick you up."

"No, I'll meet you there. I could use the walk."

"At Cascade Café?"

"Sounds good."

"Okay, I'll see you then." He hung up the

phone.

She sorted through her closet. For the first time in some time she was concerned about what to wear. It felt a little immature to pick through skirts and tops that she thought she might look nice in, but what was the harm? She selected a flowery skirt and a fitted blouse. It wasn't exactly her normal apparel, but it was nice to dress up now and then. She applied a little more makeup than normal then walked out into the kitchen. Cashew ran out after her, expecting breakfast. She was surprised when she found it already in her dish.

On the table was a note from her grandfather that detailed his plan to spend the morning house-hunting. She breathed a sigh of relief at the thought. As much as she enjoyed getting to know her grandfather, she didn't think that living with him was a good idea.

When Kerri arrived at the café Steve was already there. He waved to her from a small table in the back. She smiled as she walked over to him.

"Morning."

"Morning." He gestured to the chair across from her. "I ordered you some coffee."

"Thanks."

"Sorry for waking you up." He smiled sheepishly as he glanced away from her.

"It's okay. I can't wait to hear what you found."

"Maybe you'd like to tell me what you found first."

"What I found?" She raised an eyebrow.

"I know about your little home invasion last night."

Kerri opened her mouth to question him more, but the waitress arrived before she could. She placed her order, then waited for Steve to place his. When the waitress walked away she met his eyes.

"How did you know?"

"I have my finger on the pulse of things

around here. So, what did you find?"

"A file with pictures of the damage to Len's house door, and a cell phone with calls to only one phone number on it."

"That's it?"

She studied him for a moment. He leaned a little closer across the table.

"There's something else, isn't there? You can trust me, Kerri."

In that moment, as she gazed into his eyes, she believed that she could. "An envelope stuffed with money."

"From the shop?"

"Maybe, I'm not sure. It was loose, there were no paper money bands around it. It would have been at least a couple of grand."

"Interesting. What did you do with it?"

"We left it there. Having the money isn't going to do anything to help the investigation, and if we were caught it would have looked like we were stealing it." She pulled a piece of paper out of her purse. "Here's the number that was called on the phone. I thought you might be able to work out who it belongs to. My grandfather tried calling it, but no one answered."

"Okay, I'll look into it right away."

"Now it's your turn." She rested her chin on her hand. "What did you find?"

"I haven't been able to confirm it, but I'm nearly certain that the woman Chris was meeting was Delores."

"His sister-in-law?" Her eyes widened. "That would be scandalous."

"And provide him even more motive."

"You're right." She cringed. "That's just awful. But you said you're not sure about it?"

"I went to a few of the shops around the hotel and questioned them about a woman that might have been seen there on the same dates that Chris flew into town. I knew it was a long shot, but I figured I would give it a try. Three people mentioned Delores."

"Wow. I never would have considered the two of them together."

"I know. But that is where we are." He shrugged. As they shared their breakfast Kerri thought about the information they had found.

"So, we're thinking that maybe Chris killed Len out of jealousy, and for the money. Maybe he was in love with Delores, saw his opportunity to have her and all of the cash, and decided to take it. But that doesn't explain why he killed Harry, or why he let me buy the store before he went in to retrieve the money. He told me that he had no idea there even was any money."

"Yes, but he might be lying. I'm not sure how Harry fits in either. But I do think that it's too much of a coincidence that Chris was in town when Harry was killed. Chris and Delores certainly can't be each other's alibi, when they both stand to profit from preventing Harry from finding that money."

Kerri finished the last bite of her eggs and took a sip of her coffee. "You're right. There's no way to eliminate Chris as a suspect, but there's also no way to prove that he was the killer."

"We're right back in an impossible situation."

"Maybe it doesn't have to be impossible. I think it's time we had a conversation with the person closest to Len, and the one who had currency bands in her pocket that match the ones we found in the shop," Kerri suggested.

"How are we going to approach that though?"

"I'm new to town. I can engage her with my charming personality." Kerri winked.

"That I don't doubt." He met her eyes with a smile. "Still, I think I should go with you."

"Why is that?" She picked up her purse.

"Because she could be dangerous."

"I think I can handle that."

"Or I could go with you." He smiled again and held her gaze. "Unless, you're opposed to spending time with me."

Kerri lowered her eyes and tried to hide a

smile. "Fine, I guess you can tag along."

"Great. I'll drive." He snatched up his keys and wallet from the table. "I'll take care of the bill and meet you outside."

"I can pay…"

"Oh stop." He rolled his eyes. "If you pay then it isn't a date." He grinned and walked towards the register. She stared after him with a half-open mouth. Was he teasing her or did he really consider their breakfast a date? She stood up and walked out of the restaurant before he could see just how red her ears were. He met her on the sidewalk and started towards the parking lot. "Ready?"

"This should be interesting." She followed him out to his car. As she suspected, he had an old Camaro. He was too adventurous to drive an average car. "How long have you had this beauty?"

He grinned at her. "You're not going to laugh at me are you?"

"No, I won't laugh."

"Since I was sixteen. It was my first car, and I haven't been able to let it go. I know that probably comes across as a little immature."

"No, I don't think so. I think it's sweet actually. I loved my first car, too. But it didn't last a year before I had to buy a new one. I guess you took much better care of yours."

"I like to spend time under the hood." He nodded. As they got into the car Kerri noticed that the interior was immaculate. She began to suspect that there was much more hidden behind those bright eyes than Steve let on. For just a moment she felt a bolt of fear. Was she alone with someone who could have been involved in Len, or Harry's murder? She glanced over at Steve as he started the car. His chiseled jawline was relaxed. Wouldn't he be a little bit nervous if he thought she was going to see through him? Or maybe he just didn't think that she was intelligent enough to accomplish that. She reminded herself to be cautious, no matter how easily he made her smile.

As he drove towards Len's house, Kerri tried to keep her composure. How would she get Delores to talk to her?

"Wait, Steve, let's go to my place first. I have a few gift baskets there, I can bring one to Delores. It will help us get in the door."

"Okay." He turned in the direction of the house. It wasn't until they pulled into her driveway that she realized she didn't have to give him any directions. A shiver crept up along her spine. He knew where she lived?

"How did you know how to get here?" She looked over at him as he turned the car off.

"It's big news when someone moves into town, especially when they buy the house that was supposed to be mine."

"Supposed to be yours?" She couldn't help but smile.

"I've had my eye on this place since I graduated from college. Of course, one of my professors lived in it then."

"I'm sorry that I stole your dream house." She frowned. "Why didn't you buy it?"

"On a reporter's salary?" He laughed and opened his door. "Not much chance of that."

Kerri stepped out of the car and smiled at the house that greeted her. "I do love coming home to this place. I thought I was so lucky when I found it. I still think I am."

"You are." He nodded. "Is your grandfather here?"

"No, he's looking at a place to rent."

"Oh, so he's not living with you?" He glanced over at her as he got out of the car.

"Just temporarily. It was a bit of a surprise actually."

"Do you know him well?"

"He is my grandfather." She stopped and turned to look at him. "I'm not sure I understand the question."

"I just mean, do you trust him?"

"More than you?" She grinned.

"I wouldn't expect you to trust me, though, I'm really not a bad guy." He smiled in return. "I just mean, people aren't always who we think they are."

"Yes, I'm starting to realize that." She started to unlock the door, but before she could a loud chatter caught her attention. "Hey there, friend." She smiled as she spotted the squirrel.

"You're friends with a squirrel?" He leaned up against the side of the house as she crouched down to greet the squirrel.

"More like he's friends with me. He likes me for some reason. Might be this." She fished in her purse and pulled out a handful of nuts, then scattered them across the ground not far from the squirrel.

"Yes, that might be it." He laughed.

The squirrel darted forward to collect the nuts. "He's a good listener."

"I am, too." He caught her eye as she stood

back up. "If you ever need someone to talk to, that is."

"Hmm, I don't know if that's safe."

"Why not?"

"I don't want to end up in the newspaper."

"Ah, funny." He smiled and tilted his head to the side in such a way that caught the sunlight. Her heart fluttered. "I'll do my best to keep your name out of it."

"Great." She fumbled with the keys and unlocked the door. When he stepped right in behind her, she panicked at what the house might look like. There were still a few boxes to unpack, and who knew how many dishes in the sink. "Sorry, for the mess."

"Oh boy, if you think this is a mess, you should definitely avoid my place."

"I'll keep that in mind." She walked over to the pantry and selected a small basket that she'd filled with nuts, nut butters, and nut brittle.

"It's just as beautiful inside as it is outside.

You made a great choice."

"I like it." She carried the basket over to the table. "Do you want a water or anything?"

"Sure, water thanks."

As she grabbed the water Cashew bolted into the kitchen and right through Steve's legs.

"Oops, that's not a squirrel."

"No, it's not." She reached down and pet the dog. "This is Cashew."

"Cashew?" He grinned. "Now, that's a perfect name."

"I thought so." She shrugged and scooped the dog up in her arms. She held out a cold bottle of water to Steve. "Just let me get her something to eat and we can head out."

"We could always bring her with us."

"What?"

"Delores has little dogs that she adores. Maybe it'll make her more friendly."

"That's a great idea. What do you think,

Cashew, want to go for a ride with us?" Cashew licked her face.

"I think that's a yes." Steve smiled.

They headed back out to the car. She set the basket in the back and held Cashew on her lap in the front.

"This is the coolest car Cashew's ever been in right, Cash?" She scratched behind her ear. The dog gave a soft bark.

"I'm glad you like it." Steve looked the dog in the eyes. "No peeing, okay?"

"Don't worry she's very well trained."

"Good, maybe she can teach my cat."

"Oh, you have a cat?'

"More like inherited. My aunt moved to a condo and they don't allow pets. She begged me to take it, and well, now she owns the place."

"Yes, cats will do that." She found it so easy to talk to Steve. Even though there was always that tiny prickle along the back of her neck when he asked too many questions or stared into her eyes too deeply, she found herself very comfortable around him.

Chapter Seventeen

Steve pulled the car into Delores' driveway. Kerri stared at the house for a moment. This was where the man who owned her shop had lived and died. It gave her an eerie sensation to look at it.

"You up for this?" Steve studied her intently.

"Sure." She smiled as Cashew licked her cheek.

She opened the car door and stepped out. Cashew barked and wagged her tail happily as she set her down on the ground and held onto her leash. Steve grabbed the basket from the backseat and together they walked up to the front door. As soon as Cashew got near the door, the dogs inside began to yap and bark. Delores opened the door and greeted them with a half-hearted smile.

"Something I can help you with?"

"Hello, Delores," Steve said.

Cashew lunged forward in an attempt to get into the house.

"Cashew, stop! I'm so sorry, she's not usually so bold."

"Look at you, aren't you just adorable." Delores crouched down and patted the top of Cashew's head. "Is she yours?"

"Yes, she is. I hear you have some of your own."

"Yes, two. They are my babies."

"I brought you a basket from my new shop. It's not open, yet, but I wanted to offer you a preview. I know that your husband previously owned the shop, and with everything going on, I just wanted to check in and see how you're doing."

"Well, it's been hard." She sighed. "Losing the love of your life is not an easy thing to recover from. Maybe in time, I'll get there."

"I guess his brother Chris has been a big support to you." Kerri smiled.

"Chris?" Delores shrugged. "I suppose. He's been kind to me." She stepped aside from the door. "Do you want to come in? You can set that basket down on the table."

"Thanks so much." Kerri stepped inside with Steve right behind her. She noticed the new wood on the door frame as she passed through it. "It's so sad about Harry, too. I hear he was very helpful in the community."

"It is sad. I can't imagine why anyone would want to kill him. But I guess that's just how it is. People die."

Her two little, furry, white dogs scampered into the kitchen to investigate Cashew. Kerri watched them close to be sure they wouldn't hurt each other.

"Yes, it's tragic, but it's true."

"Steve, I see you've gotten to know our new neighbor."

"Yes, you know I try to know everyone in town, make sure that they feel welcome." He patted Kerri's shoulder.

"I know you make it your business to know everyone's business." Delores quirked a brow.

"That's quite an interesting way to make money."

"Well, everybody has to make a living, right?" He smiled. "This is my way."

"Is that why you're here? To find out more information about the murder?" Delores asked.

"No, like I said, I just wanted to check up on you. If there's anything you need, help around the house, or just someone to talk to, I'm available." Kerri set the basket down on the counter.

"If Chris isn't." Steve offered his words in a casual tone.

"Just what is that supposed to mean, Steven?" Delores settled her gaze on him. "Would you like to come out with what you're accusing me of?"

"I'm not accusing you of anything. I just know that you and Chris are close. It's natural to seek comfort after a loss."

"Whatever you're implying is quite rude." She huffed and shook her head. "And I don't need anyone's help. I can take care of myself."

"No one is saying you can't." Kerri shot a glare

in Steve's direction. "I'm sorry. We came here with good intentions and I can see that we've upset you."

"That's to be expected." She clenched her hands at her sides. "Everyone thinks it's their business when someone dies. Do I feel guilty about my husband's death? Of course I do. If I had just stayed home, or come home earlier then I might have been able to protect him."

"I'm so sorry, Delores. It's an awful thing to experience. But you have to know it wasn't your fault. Len would have wanted to protect you when the murderer broke in."

"Yes, probably." She sniffled. "He was a good man."

"But you must have been fed up with him. I mean he was a criminal? He couldn't have been easy to live with." Steve set his jaw as he locked eyes with her. "How many times did you have to bail him out, Delores?"

"I don't like what you're implying, Steven. We'd moved past all that. Yes, Len liked fast money, and he committed crimes, but he was just misunderstood. It took me a long time to work out how to get along with him, but once I did we were just fine."

"Of course you were," Kerri said trying to relieve the tension. "Once again I'm sorry for your loss."

"Thank you, but I think I've had enough of this visit. You can both leave." She jabbed her finger towards the door. "And take that little mutt with you."

Kerri gasped at her words and reached down to pick up Cashew who was in an epic battle with one of the other dogs over a little package on the floor. She held her close as she hurried out the door of the house. Steve followed after her.

"I'm going to walk home," she said as she walked faster, right past his car.

"Kerri! Wait, why?" Steve chased after her. "Get in the car, I'll take you home."

"No, thank you, I prefer walking."

"Kerri." He caught up with her and curled his hand around her elbow. "What's wrong?"

"What was that stunt back there? We were just supposed to be talking to her, not attacking her."

"It was the only way I thought I could get her to talk. She wasn't exactly volunteering information."

"She's a grieving widow."

"Who meets her late husband's brother for romantic encounters. Remember? She tried to act like she loved Len so much. So much that she was having an affair with his brother?"

"We don't know if it was definitely Delores that Chris was meeting. If it was Delores, we don't know when that started. She could have turned to Chris for comfort after Len's death. Or they could just be friends with each other. Maybe they were meeting for other reasons."

"I just think that Delores is lying about her affection for Len."

"That doesn't make her a murderer though. Relationships can be complicated. Even though he was always in trouble and their lives had to be pretty chaotic, maybe deep down she wanted to be with him and didn't care about the rest. We can't know for sure what's in her heart."

"You are right about that, I know that. But I could just tell that she was lying. We can't let this drag on forever, can we?"

Kerri shook her head and looked down at Cashew in her arms. "No, we can't. If I don't get my shop open soon I'm probably going to have to give up and salvage what money I can."

"Don't do that." He shook his head and scratched the top of Cashew's head. "I wish that our encounter with Delores was more fruitful. It didn't give us any new information."

"I know." Kerri sighed and pulled the little package out of Cashew's mouth that she had won from the other dogs. Cashew growled and wriggled, but let it go. Kerri looked at it and noticed it was a small, wrapped biscuit.

"Let me take you home, Kerri."

"It's okay. I could use the walk. It's not far, and I want to sort some things out in my mind."

"All right. I hope." He paused and met her eyes again. "I know I've been strange around you. It's just that you make me feel strange."

"I do?" She laughed a little. "How?"

"I don't know exactly. I've never met a person like you before, so determined to get answers. It reminds me of me."

"Steve, I don't think you're strange. Far from it." She held his gaze for a moment as her cheeks flushed. "I should get going. Thanks for all of your help."

She set Cashew down to let her walk. When she glanced back over her shoulder she noticed Steve getting into his car.

As Kerri walked back to her house she tried to fit the pieces together. From what they could tell Chris was sleeping with Delores. Len was a criminal that would do anything for a quick buck.

Frankie was at the shop close to the time Harry was killed, and was once Len's partner in crime. Harry was a kind handyman who was more interested in helping others than doing anything to hurt them. Then there was Detective Meyers, who appeared to be Chief Higgins' puppet. How was he involved in all of this?

As Kerri passed a trashcan she stopped to drop the biscuit that Cashew won from the other dogs into the trash. As it dropped into the container she noticed a logo on it. Her heart jumped. There it was, the same logo that was on the back of the envelope stuffed with money that she had found in Harry's house. She checked her phone to be sure. In the picture on her phone the logo was smudged, but it was clear to her that they matched. As she looked at the logo she suddenly remembered where she had seen it before. The Vuebelle Hotel. The biscuit was from the hotel so that meant that the envelope was from the hotel. Of course Delores could have an envelope from there if she was meeting Chris there, but how did the envelope end up in Harry's house, and why was it filled with money?

As Kerri continued to walk she noticed a broken bottle on the floor. She pulled Cashew's leash to the side so she wouldn't step in the glass. As she did Harry's conversation with the locksmith floated back through her mind.

"Delores was worried about her dogs being outside, because their paws might be cut by the glass," she said to herself as her eyes widened. "But if the glass was on the outside of the window that means that someone broke it from the inside. Why would anyone do that?" She thought about it more as she made her way back to the house. The person who broke it wanted to make it look like a break-in!

As Kerri reached her driveway her cell phone rang. She saw it was Steve and she picked it up.

"Kerri, I just wanted to let you know that I've finally traced the number called from Harry's cell phone."

"And?" Kerri asked.

"It is a phone registered to Delores." That little bit of information added to the suspicions she had. Maybe Harry was just discussing the broken door with Delores? Or maybe he just wanted to know what had happened? Was Harry calling Delores because he suspected her of being her husband's killer? But was she?

"Wow, that certainly makes things more interesting."

"Oh, I have another call. I'll catch up with you later."

"Okay thanks, Steve." Kerri ended the call as she reached her house.

Once inside Kerri looked at the pictures of the door frame they took from Harry's house. Her stomach flipped as the pieces began to finally fit. Harry knew the glass was wrong, and that the door frame wasn't quite right either. Maybe he suspected that it was literally an inside job. Someone had broken the door open from the inside. Just like the window was shattered from the inside. No criminal breaking into the house was going to do that. Which meant that Len was murdered by someone who wanted to make it look like a botched robbery. Someone who probably knew him. Someone who stood to profit from his death.

Had Harry figured it out? Did he decide instead of going to the cops he would confront Delores with the information? Did he maybe decide to blackmail Delores? Is that where the money came from in Harry's house? As the theory formed in her mind she couldn't quite believe it. Maybe Delores lied about her relationship with Chris, but was she really capable of killing her husband and Harry? If the window and the door were broken from the inside, how did the police not notice this? Or maybe they did and someone on the force was involved in the cover-up. Was it Detective Meyers, or the chief, or someone else entirely?

She picked up her cell phone and held it tight in her hand. She could call Steve to run the theory by him. She could call her grandfather and ask

241

him for his advice. Or she could just go back to Delores' house and find out the truth once and for all. Even if she wasn't the murderer she might know who was. She could ask Steve or her grandfather to come with her, but she thought she would have the best chance of finding out the truth if she was alone. She couldn't go to the police because she didn't know who she could trust and she didn't know if they would do anything about it. It was just a hunch after all. If Delores wasn't the murderer she might be more forthcoming with information if Kerri was alone. Kerri gave Cashew a kiss on the top of her head, then left the house.

Chapter Eighteen

As Kerri drove back towards Delores' house she recited in her mind what she would say to her. She couldn't accuse her of the murder, but if she sympathized with her she might open up about what she knew.

There was still the possibility that someone from the police force was the murderer and they were trying to cover it up. It was still possible that Chris was behind it all. Maybe he had killed Len because of his dodgy business dealings, or maybe he wanted the money, or because he wanted Delores for himself. Then he killed Harry because he had figured out the truth. Or maybe to stop Harry blackmailing him? Or even to stop him from blackmailing Delores? Maybe Delores knew that Chris had killed her husband? Maybe she even caught him in the act? Maybe she was even covering up for him?

Kerri parked a few houses away from Delores' house to give herself some time to think things through. As she started to walk towards Delores' driveway she noticed another car in it.

She wasn't sure who the car belonged to. Instead of walking up to the door she hung back near a tree and waited to see what might unfold. After a few minutes she heard some raised voices from inside the house. Her heartbeat quickened as the voices sounded quite angry. She edged her way up to the house and peeked into the front window. She couldn't see either person inside, but their voices were much louder. One was gruff, and vaguely familiar, the other belonged to Delores.

"I trusted you!"

"And so did I! You were supposed to protect me! But you weren't there, were you?" Delores' voice was shrill.

"Don't you turn this around on me. You conned me into believing that you were attacked by Len because of me. I know now that you weren't," the man said gruffly.

"You don't know that. All you know is that you're feeling guilty. You have no reason to be. I

244

will take care of you. If you just calm down, and think this through, you'll see that there's no reason to panic. Everything is as it should be."

"I don't need you to take care of me. You've ruined my life. Nothing is as it should be."

"You need someone to take care of you, that's for sure. Let's be honest about why you helped me. You helped me because you wanted to be with me, didn't you? You thought you were in love with me?" Delores said.

"Stop it, that's not true. I thought you were a victim who needed my help. My judgment was clouded and I did something terrible." Kerri tried to figure out who the voice belonged to. Was it Chris?

"No? I'm not good enough for you?" Delores laughed sarcastically. "I doubt that. You wanted me, you just didn't want to admit it."

"I wanted to take the criminals out of our town, that's all I wanted. You were helping me with that and I thought I had put you in danger so I wanted to protect you." Kerri still couldn't work out who was talking to Delores, was it Detective Meyers?

"And you did. I just needed to take care of a few loose ends, that's all. Now that they're tied up, you can breathe easy."

"Loose ends, you killed Harry in cold blood."

"He had worked out what I had done. I did what had to be done to protect us both."

"The truth will be told."

"No one is ever going to hear the truth from me."

"Disgusting. I will never allow that. Even if it means I go to prison, I will make sure that the truth is known."

Kerri held her breath as she knew those words were a direct threat against a woman who appeared to be more dangerous than she ever could have imagined. She was about to duck back into hiding when the front door flew open, and Chief Higgins started to step out onto the front porch. Kerri locked eyes with him just before he was yanked back into the house. She didn't hesitate to lunge after him. As soon as she was past the threshold she froze. Delores clutched a gun in her hand which she pointed directly at Chief Higgins.

"Don't you move a muscle, either of you, or I will pull the trigger."

Kerri raised her hands slowly into the air. "You don't have to do this, Delores." She aimed the gun straight at Kerri's chest. Kerri's heart skipped and her breath left her, as if she'd already been shot. Of all the things she expected, she didn't even consider that Delores might be armed. That had probably been Harry's downfall as well. He never expected Delores, soft-spoken and apparently kind, to be as cut-throat as she was.

"Don't tell me what I don't have to do. Close the door." She shifted the gun towards Kerri for just a second, then pointed it back at Chief Higgins. "Do you see what you've done now? A man of the law." She shook her head. "Now we're in a real mess. All you had to do was play along and everyone's lives would have continued on, no worse off than they are now."

"No worse? What about Harry's poor parents?" Chief Higgins asked.

Delores waved her hand and shrugged. "They'll move on eventually."

"Whatever has happened here, Delores, we can still fix it. Just take a breath and think about what you're doing. Put down the gun, and back away," Kerri said.

"No, the time for fixing things has passed. I'm sorry you stumbled into this mess, Kerri, but here you are. I've worked too hard to get what I want. It has not been easy. Harry thought he was so clever by trying to blackmail me with the pictures of the door and the broken glass. He thought he was going to score big because he was too nosy to leave things alone. He got what was coming to him." She took a step closer to the chief and smiled. "And so will you."

"What could you have against the chief?" Kerri asked. She was intrigued and maybe if

Delores was talking it would calm the situation down.

"I didn't have anything against him. I spoon-fed him every little detail that would lead him to arrest Chris. Even though he was innocent in all of this. When I needed to get rid of my husband, he played right along to keep me out of jail. I had Chief Higgins wrapped around my little finger. He knew what I'd done, but I convinced him I did it in self-defense. I conned him into thinking that Len tried to kill me, because he found out that I was helping the chief. He swept it under the rug for me, because he thought I was a damsel in distress. He also felt guilty for putting me in that position. He never thought that a woman like me could wrap a sander cord around a man's neck and kill him in cold blood so he never suspected that I killed Harry. Up until now he thought that Chris or one of Len's criminal friends killed Harry. So now I have to take care of the problem."

"You don't have to do this," Kerri pleaded. She realized how Chief Higgins was involved in the cover-up of Len's death. He wasn't paid off, or blackmailed into it. He did it because he had sympathy for a woman he thought he put in a dangerous situation.

"But now, he's grown a conscience. Haven't you, Higgins?" She looked down the gun at him.

"I just want the truth to be revealed, Delores. That's why I came here. I never wanted to hurt anyone, you're the one that did those things, not me," Chief Higgins said.

"Well, you have the truth now. I'm no one's victim. I wanted that money, and I was going to get it. Then Harry tried to take it from me, so I took care of him, too. Now, you're going to try to arrest me, and I'm going to have to stop you. But that's not what it will look like. I will be sure to let everyone know how you killed Len and expected me to do whatever you asked to cover it up."

"You're not going to get away with this. People know that I'm here and they will come looking for me," Kerri said.

"And they will find you. But it will be too late.

You will be shot by dear old Chief Higgins. Maybe he was too stressed and didn't see who you were, or maybe he was upset that you interrupted our little tryst, it doesn't matter. Because he's going to shoot you with his gun, which will give Detective Meyers all the proof he needs to wrap this tragedy up."

"I'll do no such thing!" Chief Higgins took a step back and raised his hands into the air.

"Oh, yes you will. Draw your gun, old man."

"I won't. You'll have to shoot me first."

"Fair enough." She shrugged. "Kerri walked in on me in the middle of a fight with you and you went after her, but I got your gun and shot you myself. In the mix the gun went off again and Kerri was shot, poor girl." Delores raised her hand and with all her force hit him across the head with her gun. He wasn't expecting it and he fell hard to the floor. He cried out and then writhed on the floor clutching his head. Kerri reached down to help him.

"Stop!" Delores shouted as she waved the gun

in Kerri's direction.

Delores reached down and grabbed the gun out of the holster on Chief Higgins' hip and pointed it at him. Kerri tried to change tactics and distract her. "I understand why you did what you did. It must have been so difficult living with a criminal all those years?"

"You might understand, but the police won't. Len liked to use me to fund his criminal behavior? Anytime I thought we were getting ahead he would bankrupt us and land in jail. Was that how I was supposed to live my life? It doesn't matter that his brother was going to take everything that I owned? The only reason he showed any interest in me was because he knew that I had the money from the business."

"So? What difference does that make? Len didn't deserve to die."

"Oh, but he did. Len had it coming. I warned him the last time he tried to hide the money from me that he would pay for it. I'm the one that set up all of the contacts. Without me he wouldn't have had anything to fence. But he was an idiot and got himself caught one too many times. Detective Meyers was on our case all the time, then Chief Higgins started sniffing around. I warned Len that he needed to let me take over. But he acted like he had the right to run my life and hide the money from me."

"That's not fair," Kerri said pretending to sympathize with the woman so she could get more information out of her.

"No, it isn't and I had to fix it like I have to fix everything." She held her head high. "So, I started feeding Chief Higgins information, only I told him that Chris was the ringleader. The more information I fed him, the more he protected me. But when Chief Higgins started to close in on Chris, Len figured it out and he wanted to protect his brother."

"And you needed to protect yourself?"

"Of course I did. The stupid fool didn't realize I was protecting him. That I was doing this for him, for us. Instead, he was furious with me. He came after me. I had no choice but to kill him. Too bad, he lied to me about where the money was before he died." She stopped talking and closed her eyes.

"You had no idea where it was?" Kerri pressed. Kerri looked towards Chief Higgins who had now stopped moving. He was out cold, she hoped that he was still alive.

"No, he lied to me." She sighed. "When you found the money, I knew it wasn't all there. Once I knew where Len had hid some of the money I remembered the loose molding and I thought he had probably hidden the rest there. So, I decided to kill two birds with one stone. Harry had worked out what I had done. I paid him to keep him quiet. But he wanted more and more money from me to keep what he knew a secret. I didn't want to have to do the work of pulling up the rest of the floorboards. So I made him a deal. If he agreed to stop hounding me about the door and the window and kept his mouth shut, I would tell him where Len had probably hid the rest of the money and split it with him. If he wasn't so greedy he wouldn't have done it, but he did. I waited until he found the money, then I did what I had to do."

"You killed him."

"I had no choice." She shrugged then her eyes narrowed as she stared at Kerri. "Let me warn you right now, Kerri, men can't be trusted. My husband was a criminal and greedy, his brother is a con artist, and Harry was only out to make a dollar. I wasn't about to let Len control me, or Chris con me, or Harry take advantage of me. I had to fight for myself, no one else was going to help me. And now I need to make sure that Chief Higgins doesn't betray me."

"We can fix this, Delores."

"You're right, now it's time to fix the problem." Delores looked towards the chief who was still lying on the floor.

"Don't do this, Delores. There are still ways that you can get out of this. All we have to do is tell the police that you were crazy with grief. You can plead insanity. You can walk away from all of this." Kerri tried everything to make the woman reconsider her actions.

Delores aimed the gun at Chief Higgins who was now awake, still writhing in pain on the floor. She released the safety. Kerri knew she had only moments to act. She lunged forward and attempted to knock the gun out of Delores' hand. She managed to move the hand that held the gun. The gun still fired and a bullet lodged in the kitchen wall. As Kerri tried to wrestle the gun away from her the front door banged open. George and Steve barreled inside. George pulled Delores off Kerri and wrenched the gun out of her hand, while Steve pulled Kerri away from the fray.

"Are you okay?" He gazed into her eyes. "We heard a gunshot."

"I'm okay, the shot hit the wall. Is the chief okay."

Steve knelt down beside him. "He'll be fine, he's just knocked out. The ambulance is on the way."

"I'm never getting married," Kerri blurted the

words out as she heard sirens blare from outside. Steve looked over at her and smiled a little.

"Can't say I blame you there."

"You'll forget about this soon enough and change your mind." George looked at her. Kerri gave them a quick rundown of what she had learned about Delores' and the chief's involvement,

Paramedics were followed by police officers and then Detective Meyers. The detective looked from the chief on the floor up to Kerri. After the paramedics loaded the chief into an ambulance Kerri gave her statement to Detective Meyers, but she was hesitant. Could he be trusted? He just questioned her as if he was going through the motions. He didn't seem surprised by what Kerri told him about the chief. Was that because he was also involved?

When the detective was finished with her Kerri walked over to Steve and her grandfather.

"How did you know to look for me?" She looked from her grandfather to Steve, then back again. "I didn't tell anyone I was coming here."

"We'll talk about that later." George's brow furrowed. "The important thing is that you're safe, and I might have installed a GPS tracker on your car."

"What?" Kerri's eyes widened. "Why would you do that?"

He rubbed the back of his neck and cringed. "I'm a little overprotective. It's been there since you graduated."

"Grandpa!"

"It served its purpose didn't it? Steve called to tell me he couldn't get hold of you and wondered if I knew where you were. We were concerned that you might have decided to go speak to Delores again." He crossed his arms.

"Lucky you found me," Kerri said.

"All that matters is that you're safe. Let's get you home." He nodded to Steve. "Thanks for your help."

"Yes, thank you," Kerri smiled slightly. "I bet

you have a great story now."

"That I do. But I wish you weren't in such a dangerous position."

"I'm fine aren't I?" Kerri's cheeks warmed as he held her gaze.

"If I had been with you..."

"I didn't want you to be with me. I didn't want anyone to be with me. I thought if I spoke to her alone she would give me information."

"You shouldn't have gone alone," George said.

"This may come as a surprise to you, Grandpa, but I am used to making my own decisions and living an independent life. You showed up and acted as if you were in charge suddenly. I'm just not accustomed to that."

George's jaw rippled as if he might lose his temper, but he took a breath and nodded. "You're right. I did come on a little strong. It's just that I've been looking forward to this time with you. This is new for me, too."

"I know it is." She smiled at him. "We'll work

it out together."

"I'll find a place to live, we could use the space I think."

"We'll figure it out, Grandpa. I'm glad you're here. The two of you came to my rescue." She looked back at Steve and smiled. "I don't know how I'll ever thank you."

"Just give me a quote." He grinned.

"Seriously?"

He shook his head and smiled. "No. Just take care of yourself. I'll be by to check on you."

She smiled at the thought. "Thanks, Steve."

As she left the house with her grandfather she glanced back over her shoulder at it. It would soon be empty. Len lost his life, and Delores lost her freedom. Maybe there was a reason for both, but it would never make sense to her. Harry's family would continue to grieve, as would the town full of people who knew him to be a good man. Maybe he'd taken advantage of the situation instead of going to the police, or maybe he doubted that the police would actually do anything to help. Either way, he didn't deserve to die. She was relieved that the chief was safe, but she also wondered just exactly how involved he was in the crimes.

Chapter Nineteen

The next morning Kerri woke up to her grandfather standing over her with a tray filled with breakfast. She had fallen asleep fully dressed on the couch. The events of the previous day had taken it out of her. She sat up and wiped at her eyes.

"Grandpa, you didn't have to do that."

"I know I didn't. But I did, so eat."

"Thank you." She accepted the tray and set it down on the coffee table. "Are you going to join me?"

"Sorry, I ate already. I can't sleep past sunrise. If you don't mind, while you eat, I'm going to go for a jog."

"You have way too much energy."

"It's important to stay healthy." He nodded to the glass of orange juice. "Drink up. I'll be back in forty minutes."

"Okay." She grinned and took a sip of her juice. Just as she finished her breakfast there was a knock on the door. Kerri glanced at her phone. No one had called to let her know they were coming over. Her heart skipped a beat at the thought that it might be Steve. That made her freeze for a moment. What was that? The start of a crush? She grimaced at the thought. As she walked towards the door, her heart pounded a little faster. She opened the door to find Detective Meyers outside.

"Kerri, I'm sorry to disturb you. Could I come in?"

She hesitated. Was Detective Meyers involved in covering up Len's murder as well. She wasn't sure how deep the cover-up ran. She wasn't sure that he could be trusted. But she didn't know how to turn him away.

"All right." She stepped aside to allow him in.

"You're a brave woman, you know that?" He stared into her eyes with a steely gaze.

She swallowed hard. "What can I help you

with, Detective?" She backed away a few steps.

"I wanted to thank you. I'm sorry you got tangled up in all of this, but if you didn't do what you did yesterday who knows what would have happened."

"I just did what I had to do. How is the chief?"

"He is still in hospital but he will be fine. He has resigned." He pulled off his hat and wiped some sweat from his temple.

"That's probably for the best."

"Yes, there is going to be an official investigation. I have known the chief for many years and I cannot believe he did this. I mean I suspected he was involved, but I could never believe it. He always seemed to have the best intentions." Was he defending the chief's actions? Her heart raced. Maybe he was involved.

"Maybe we should talk about this later. I need to get back to something in the kitchen."

"Wait, Kerri." He caught her by the elbow. "You should know this." Kerri's heart raced as she turned back to face him. Had she put herself in danger yet again? He released her elbow and turned away. "The chief admitted to knowing that Delores killed Len. Apparently he thought it was his fault. He was pushing her for information about her husband's crimes, and Len found out and attacked her. They fought because she was feeding him lies about Chris, and the chief was about to arrest Chris. Chief Higgins thought Delores was attacked by Len because of him. He knew that if he didn't protect her, she wouldn't testify against Chris, so he helped cover it up." He closed his eyes. "Apparently, she called him that night and said that someone had broken in and killed Len. He was the first on the scene and he could see that it wasn't a break-in straight away. He asked her and she told him that Len attacked her, that she defended herself. She was terrified that she was going to jail for it." He wiped his hand across his face and groaned. "Chief Higgins felt so guilty that he covered up a murder. Because of that, Harry was killed, and you were put in danger."

"How was Chris involved in all of this?"

"He wasn't involved in any of it. He found out that Len was involved in fencing so he pulled out of the business. He was meeting Delores at the hotel to try and sort out the financial matters of the business and Len's estate. Chris is shocked by all of this. He is apparently in a relationship with his friend's ex-wife and she preferred to keep it a secret so he was meeting her at the hotel. Delores has given us a full statement for a reduced sentence and she has admitted that he wasn't involved at all."

"I thought he was innocent," Kerri said.

"The chief put a lot of pressure on me to let the cases go cold. I tried to resist him. But I wish I had done more. For that I'm very sorry, Kerri. I hope this entire experience won't turn you off our town."

"No, it hasn't. Thanks for stopping by, Detective."

"At least now you don't have to worry about snooping around anymore." He nodded at her then turned and walked out of the house. As she watched him go she felt a sense of relief. Maybe Chief Higgins had been involved in the cover-up and maybe the detective could have done more, but they both seemed to have a desire to protect the town.

As his car pulled out of the driveway, another pulled in.

Natalie grinned as she popped out of the car with a bag of doughnuts and two coffees.

"Morning, Boss."

"I told you not to call me that." Kerri laughed.

"I'm just glad I still get to."

"I'm glad you're here. I need your help." Kerri pulled her into the house.

A few hours later Steve knocked on the door. Kerri opened the door and smiled.

"Thanks for stopping by."

"What is that delicious smell?" He walked right past her into the house. "Whatever it is, I have to have some, right now."

"Good timing, I just took it out of the oven." She laughed as she led him into the kitchen where Natalie and George were already seated at the table. "This recipe is one I learned from my grandmother." She smiled as she set the maple nut pie in the middle of the table. "She made it every year for Thanksgiving, even if we couldn't all be together."

"Yes, she did." George groaned as he rubbed his stomach. "I have been longing for that pie for a long time."

"Let's dig in." Kerri grinned as she began to slice up the pie. She caught Steve gazing in her direction. Her heart skipped a beat. She slid the pie onto a plate and handed it to him. "I hope you like it. It's my way of saying thank you, to all of you, for making this transition to a new home a wonderful one. Thanks for helping me make the pie, Nat."

"Oh, this is so good." Natalie sighed as she took her first bite. "I know where I'm going to be for Thanksgiving."

Kerri laughed. As she watched her friends and her grandfather enjoy their pie, it struck her that this was exactly where she wanted to be. She'd finally found the family she'd been looking for most of her life. She'd finally found a home. She was looking forward to opening the shop and the adventures that the future held.

The End

Toasted Pecan Cookie Recipe

Ingredients:

1 cup pecans

4 ounces softened butter

1/2 cup light brown sugar

1 large egg at room temperature

1 teaspoon vanilla extract

1 cup all-purpose flour

1/8 teaspoon salt

Preparation:

Preheat the oven to 350 degrees Fahrenheit.

Place the pecans on a baking tray lined with parchment paper and place in the preheated oven for 4-5 minutes, until the nuts are lightly toasted. Once toasted leave aside to cool. Once cooled roughly chop the nuts.

Place parchment paper on cookie trays.

Cream the butter and sugar with an electric mixer.

Gradually add the egg to the mixture, beating until well-combined. Mix in the vanilla extract.

Sift the flour and salt into a separate bowl.

Gradually add the flour mixture to the egg mixture and stir until well-combined.

Stir the chopped pecans into the mixture.

Cover the batter and leave in the fridge to cool for about an hour.

Roll the cooled mixture into balls about the size of a tablespoon and place on the cookie trays about 2 inches apart. Flatten the balls slightly. This recipe makes about 24 cookies.

Bake for about 10-12 minutes and then remove from the oven. The cookies will be soft, but will continue cooking while they cool.

Leave to cool on the tray for about 10 minutes

then transfer to a wire rack to cool completely.

Enjoy!

Maple Nut Pie Recipe

Ingredients:

Pastry:

1 1/4 cups all-purpose flour

Pinch of salt

2 tablespoons superfine sugar

1/2 cup (1 stick) cold unsalted butter

2-3 tablespoons iced water

Nut filling:

2/3 cup pecans

2/3 cup walnuts

2/3 cup macadamia nuts

3/4 cup pure maple syrup

2 ounces butter

1 tablespoon all-purpose flour

2 tablespoons light brown sugar

1/8 teaspoon salt

3 eggs

Preparation:

You will need 1 nine inch tart pan with a removable bottom.

For the pastry sift the flour and salt into a large bowl. Mix in the sugar.

Add the cubed, cold butter to the bowl with the flour mixture. Rub the flour mixture and butter together using your fingertips until the butter is incorporated and the mixture is crumbly. Don't overwork the mixture.

Gradually add some of the iced water to the mixture until the mixture forms a dough.

Wrap the dough in plastic wrap and put it in the fridge for about 30 minutes.

When the pastry is cold preheat the oven to 350 degrees Fahrenheit. Grease and flour the tart pan.

Take the cooled pastry out of the fridge. On a floured surface using a floured rolling pin roll the pastry into a circular shape until about 1/4 of an inch thick. Press into tart pan and remove excess pastry from the sides.

Prick the bottom and sides of the pastry with a fork and then place the pan in the fridge for about ten minutes.

Remove from the fridge and line the tart with parchment paper and baking beads. Place in the oven on the middle rack and bake for about 10 minutes. Remove the parchment paper and beads and bake the shell for another 5 minutes, or until the shell is crispy and cooked through. Once cooked put aside to cool.

While the tarts are cooking you can start on the nut filling. Take the nuts and lay them on a baking tray lined with parchment paper. Place in the pre-heated oven and toast for about 4-5 minutes. Once the nuts are toasted remove them from the oven and reduce the oven temperature to 320 degrees Fahrenheit.

In a saucepan add the maple syrup, butter, flour, sugar and salt. Gently heat the mixture until the butter is melted. Remove from the heat and leave to cool for about 5 minutes. In a bowl beat the eggs until combined. Add the cooled sugar mixture to the eggs.

Chop the cooled nuts into pieces and then add to the maple syrup mixture. Stir through thoroughly.

Pour the cooled mixture into the cooled pastry.

Place in the oven and cook for about 30-40 minutes until the mixture is set.

Take out of the oven and let it cool completely on a cooling rack and then gently remove from the tart pan.

Enjoy!

More Cozy Mysteries by Cindy Bell

Chocolate Centered Cozy Mysteries

The Sweet Smell of Murder

A Deadly Delicious Delivery

A Bitter Sweet Murder

A Treacherous Tasty Trail

Luscious Pastry at a Lethal Party

Trouble and Treats

Sage Gardens Cozy Mysteries

Birthdays Can Be Deadly

Money Can Be Deadly

Trust Can Be Deadly

Ties Can Be Deadly

Rocks Can Be Deadly

Dune House Cozy Mysteries

Seaside Secrets

Boats and Bad Guys

Treasured History

Hidden Hideaways

Dodgy Dealings

Suspects and Surprises

Wendy the Wedding Planner Cozy Mysteries

Matrimony, Money and Murder

Chefs, Ceremonies and Crimes

Knives and Nuptials

Mice, Marriage and Murder

Heavenly Highland Inn Cozy Mysteries

Murdering the Roses

Dead in the Daisies

Killing the Carnations

Drowning the Daffodils

Suffocating the Sunflowers

Books, Bullets and Blooms

A Deadly serious Gardening Contest

A Bridal Bouquet and a Body

Digging for Dirt

Bekki the Beautician Cozy Mysteries

Hairspray and Homicide

A Dyed Blonde and a Dead Body

Mascara and Murder

Pageant and Poison

Conditioner and a Corpse

Mistletoe, Makeup and Murder

Hairpin, Hair Dryer and Homicide

Blush, a Bride and a Body

Shampoo and a Stiff

Cosmetics, a Cruise and a Killer

Lipstick, a Long Iron and Lifeless

Camping, Concealer and Criminals

Treated and Dyed

Made in the USA
Middletown, DE
28 October 2016